MIDNIGHT, GHOSTS, AND GOLD!

Bernard Luthi

ISBN-13: 9781500800765
ISBN-10: 1500800767
Library of Congress Control Number: 2015912316
CreateSpace Independent Publishing Platform
North Charleston, South Carolina

For Rose, Joshua, and Jacob

CONTENTS

A true adventure doesn't require a ticket—only your imagination and willingness to go along for the ride.

Bernard Luthi

1

WAITING

The second hand on the small, round-faced clock on the dresser completed a full sweep.

It was 11:02 p.m.—another fifty-eight minutes to midnight, Andrew calculated.

He fidgeted in his bed and turned on his side. It was impossible to sleep with visions of long-lost treasures, gold, ghosts, and the walking dead flashing through his now fully alert mind.

They had planned for this night for months, carefully laying the groundwork, making lists of the supplies they would need, drawing maps, charting their course, agreeing on hand and voice signals for specific actions, and planning escape routes. They reviewed their plans, made changes, and reviewed again until they were sure they had it right, but even now, as he lay in his bed, Andrew was sure that they had forgotten something—something important.

Everything had to be perfect.

Andrew and his three best friends—Michael, William, and Daniel—were set to embark on the most adventurous night of their lives. It wasn't every day that a group of twelve-year-old boys would enter a house known to be haunted to search for lost treasure.

The boys had picked Thursday night to carry out their mission. Weekend nights were too busy—traffic in the neighborhood was heavier because people went out, and their parents often stayed up late to watch television, play cards, and entertain friends. Besides, Fridays were usually easy days at school, and if they were tired after the mission, they could catch up on sleep on Saturday, which was just around the corner. Thursday was perfect.

He glanced at the clock; it was 11:07 p.m. Another fifty-three minutes to go.

Andrew heard a noise in the house. He sat up in his bed and listened to the sound of footsteps in the hall. He saw a faint glimmer of light under his bedroom door and heard the squeak of hinges. Bathroom door, he thought. It was probably just Dad.

Andrew liked his father. They were friends. They went camping, watched sports on TV, and hung out often.

His father spoke to him as if he was a man, and that made Andrew feel good. Sure, sometimes Dad would get mad at him for things he forgot to do or ground him for missing or incomplete homework or poor grades, but it was never as bad as it was for his friend Daniel. *His* dad always seemed to be angry, and he punished Daniel for even the smallest mistakes.

Andrew's family had moved to the city of Telane from Los Angeles when he was seven.

The magazine that employed Andrew's father in Los Angeles had closed its doors permanently. When a job opportunity surfaced at the small-town newspaper, the *Telane Tribune*, Andrew, his parents, and his younger sister and brother packed up, sold their small yellow house with the wooden swing set in the backyard, and moved north to Oregon.

Andrew's father was a struggling novelist at heart. Although talented, he often left book projects unfinished, and when he did finish a project, he was reluctant to make a real attempt to get it published, using the excuse that the piece still needed work and that he would let it rest awhile before making revisions.

His father's study was full of stacks of unfinished books, short stories, and articles. Every so often, Andrew would explore his father's study and read pages from the various stacks of papers. He enjoyed his father's tales of mystery and suspense and even told his father once that he had read some of them. His father had just smiled and asked him to be careful not to rearrange or misplace any pages.

Andrew's mom was the kind of woman who always seemed to be helping people, whether it was spending time at Andrew's school or his brother and sister's school, getting involved in the church's charity events or even visiting older residents of Telane who lived alone and sometimes needed checking up on.

Andrew admired his mom, and the fact that nothing ever seemed to rattle her—especially with his younger brother and sister—was a real achievement.

Andrew's brother and sister weren't as affected by the move as he was. While they missed their friends and the old neighborhood, they had been excited at the prospect of moving to a new town.

Andrew remembered the day when his mom and dad first told him that they would be moving to Telane. He remembered feeling sad at the loss of his school friends and wondering if he would make new friends in his new city. But he trusted his dad, and his dad had told him that everything would work out fine.

Telane, a small city located on the Oregon coast near the Washington border, was not the greatest place to live, but Andrew made new friends and slowly adjusted to living in a small, quiet town.

Telane, once a booming gold-mining town, had become run-down and depressed when the mining industry collapsed. Now townspeople tried to attract tourists who wanted to fish in the ocean or camp in the vast woodlands nearby.

Before the gold rush that attracted settlers from the East Coast in the 1800s, Telane, like many towns on the

West Coast, was home to a small tribe of American Indians who played an important role in the city's history and development. The town still had a sizable American Indian population.

The townspeople were very proud of their city and its history, and the older citizens would often talk about the good old days when mines brought in big business, which, in turn, brought in big money.

Then it all came to an abrupt halt. The mines stopped producing gold, and Telane's decline was almost immediate. It was as if someone had turned off the faucet that poured gold into the mines. When new opportunities were discovered five hundred miles south in Rosemead, investors moved there, leaving Telane with unfinished construction projects and debt.

Forever the optimist, Andrew's father would say, "This town is going to put itself on the map someday. I can feel it." Andrew believed his father.

Aside from pickup baseball games and the occasional city matchup, there wasn't much for kids to do in Telane. Andrew would hang out with his friends after school or occasionally visit his dad at the *Tribune* to hear news of break-ins or fights down at the dock that he could share with his friends before the next morning's paper came out.

Andrew's father had a great imagination and a sense of adventure—so much so that when he received a call one Saturday morning about two men who had spent a lot of money on shovels, picks, flashlights, batteries, and supplies at the local hardware store, he stopped working on his book and immediately left the house to ferret out the story.

It wasn't unusual for prospectors to show up from time to time, since it was a known fact that old mines sometimes yielded gold for those willing to dig just a little deeper or those who were lucky enough to apply their picks in just the right spot. The odd thing about these two men was that they bought their digging supplies in town, which indicated that they were probably not experienced gold hunters. More likely, they were novices visiting Telane for a weekend gold exploration. Then again, maybe—just maybe—someone had found gold!

After much discussion, it became clear that nobody knew who these men were or what they were up to. Andrew's father made the story as interesting as possible by speculating that someone might have found a good mine up in the mountains. His headline in the *Tribune* the next morning read, "Strangers to Spark Second Gold Rush?" That day, the *Tribune* sold a lot of newspapers.

It was 11:11 p.m. Andrew decided to get up and get ready at 11:45 p.m. It would only take him two minutes to get his things together and another ten minutes to pick up Daniel at his house before meeting the other boys behind Michael's house.

Michael was the first friend Andrew had made when he moved to Telane. Andrew had always been a little on the shy side; halfway through his first day at school, he'd uttered little more than a quiet yes or no to a teacher. During lunch, he was sitting by himself when someone called out, "Hey, new kid." When Andrew turned to look around, he saw Michael sitting at the next table with a few other boys. He was roughly Andrew's height. Although he was thin, he was muscular. He had short, wavy brown hair; dark eyes; and just the hint of freckles on his light skin. "You want to sit with us?" asked Michael. Andrew agreed and moved to Michael's table, and the boys quickly became best friends.

Michael was the opposite of Andrew. He was restless, outspoken, defiant, and quick to get into arguments and fights with other boys. He even occasionally talked back to teachers, which earned him detentions at school. He enjoyed sports and was good at them. He could run faster than anyone else could at school.

Michael lived with his mother and two sisters three blocks away. His father had died when he was four, and he once told Andrew that he could only remember a few things about his father, but he remembered that he liked him. Michael didn't talk much about his dad and how he died. Only once did he share with Andrew the few things he remembered and the fact that he missed his father.

The outside walls of Michael's house were full of cracks, and the paint on the window frames and door was peeling. The picket fence that surrounded the house was missing several planks of wood, and the once-bright brick walkway was chipped and dull. Weeds replaced the colorful flowers that once decorated the front of the house. Michael would always tell the boys that he was going to fix up the house someday; he just needed some money. Andrew figured that Michael was embarrassed by his house; if he hadn't brought up its condition, the other boys probably wouldn't have noticed.

Andrew liked Michael's mom. She always offered the boys something to drink and eat when they came over, and she smiled often, although Andrew thought she always looked tired and worried.

Michael often talked about the things he would do when his family saved some money. They'd go on a vacation to Hawaii, get a new dirt bike, or fix his father's motorcycle, which leaned up against the back of Michael's garage. Andrew believed him. Michael was his best friend. They spent many hours together, talking about how they would get cars when they got their driver's permits and how they would both become famous someday. Andrew was going to be a baseball player, and Michael was going to be an explorer, like the people on Discovery Channel who ventured into the Amazon basin or the Australian outback. Both boys would become famous for their achievements and receive worldwide acclaim and the riches that went along with it.

They picked Michael's house to rendezvous for the start of their mission for two reasons: First, it was perfectly located. Its large backyard abutted the dry riverbed they'd use to make their trip to the haunted house virtually unnoticed by anyone else. Second, Michael's mother and older sister worked the late shift at the local hospital, giving the boys a place to plan and even set up the first stage of their mission without interruption or discovery.

At 11:15 p.m., Andrew tossed and turned in his bed. "This is taking way too long," he agonized. Months of planning had seemed to fly by, but now this last hour was taking an eternity. Andrew lay in his bed and visualized finding strongboxes of treasure hidden in the basement of the Wilson family's haunted mansion. He remembered the excitement they'd all felt when he and Michael told the other two boys about the old map they found sealed under the lining of an old footlocker in Michael's attic.

The footlocker had belonged to Michael's great-great-grandfather, Theodore Wilson. It had been given to Michael's dad when his father, Daniel Wilson, passed away. The footlocker contained many seemingly worthless odds and ends, and Michael's father put it up in the attic shortly after he received it.

The last-known resident of the haunted mansion was John Wilson, more commonly referred to in the local legend as "Old Man Wilson." He lived in the mansion for about fifty years, until he disappeared some ten years back. There were many rumors about what happened to Old Man Wilson; the neighborhood favorite was that he had died deep under the mansion in one of the tunnels he had dug while looking for long-lost gold, and now his ghost patrolled the house, scaring off anyone who came to steal his treasure.

Michael and Andrew had found the map while searching the attic one afternoon out of boredom. Michael's attic was full of old suitcases, footlockers, and storage boxes that had been passed down over the years by various family members. Most had come from Michael's great-uncles and were stuffed with old clothes, books, and odds and ends.

The boys had been looking for an old watch Michael recalled seeing. He figured he could sell it for a few dollars. As he dug through the footlocker, he noticed that the lining on the bottom stuck up in one corner. After one quick tug, Michael could see that it concealed a small hiding place, which contained the map.

Michael had stared at the map with a blank face and then turned to Andrew, who had stood there with an open mouth and wide eyes. They knew they had found something special.

The document was a large piece of parchment paper, torn, tattered, and yellow with age. On it were detailed drawings of the interior of a large house and its first floor and basement.

A large arrow pointed to an area of the basement labeled "subbasement."

Under that arrow were the words "Far left corner of room, down."

In another corner of the parchment, there was a drawing of what appeared to be a cave. Under this sketch were the words "Two tunnels. Go left, left again, left again, right."

Below this was an illustration of a room, with the words "Standing in room center, look up, use imagination."

Finally, in all four corners of the parchment were circular designs.

"Is that what I think it is?" asked Andrew.

"I think so," responded Michael. "I think it's a map of the Wilson mansion and what's beneath it."

Whoever created the map must have thought that someone else might use it eventually—hence the command "Use imagination." If the map had been for the creator's use only, then it would have simply stated where the gold was. The boys spent many hours pondering this puzzle and finally agreed that Theodore Wilson must have created the map for his sons. It was possible that Theodore had created the map but never had a chance to give it to his sons, who had left home long before Theodore died unexpectedly after a bad fall.

Well, this was all the boys needed. There was gold in that mansion, and they were going to find it—ghosts or not!

2

ON THE MOVE

At 11:40 p.m., Andrew slid from his bed and put on his black jeans. It was close enough to midnight. He slid on a black Oakland Raiders T-shirt and a black sweatshirt and pulled a dark-blue beanie over his head.

It was important to dress dark—better for blending in with the night; Andrew and the boys had agreed to it the day before.

Andrew quickly put on his shoes and pulled the backpack stuffed with supplies out of the closet.

"Now the tricky part," he whispered to himself as he opened his bedroom window and quietly climbed onto the roof of his old two-story house.

He slid the window three-quarters closed, walked gingerly to the edge of the roof, quietly lowered himself by holding onto a rain gutter, and stepped onto the extended branch of the large oak tree that grew on the side of the house. From the branch, it was quick work to swing himself onto a lower branch and then drop to the grass below. Once he hit the ground, Andrew began jogging toward Daniel's house, which was a couple of blocks away. As he began to jog, he looked over his shoulder at his house to be sure that no lights had come on, indicating that he had been heard.

As he neared Daniel's house, Andrew could make out a figure in the distance. Andrew darted behind some bushes, fearing that the figure was a neighbor coming home late from work—or worse, a police officer on patrol. He peered through the branches of the bush and could see the figure pacing back and forth. It was Daniel! Relieved, Andrew leaped out from behind his hiding spot and continued toward his friend.

"I couldn't sleep," whispered Daniel.

"Me neither," replied Andrew.

Without further words, the two boys started out toward Michael's house.

Daniel was the first boy Andrew met when he arrived in Telane. Daniel was a quiet, timid boy who was small for his age and rather thin. His light-brown hair was cut short and neatly combed to the side. He had sharp features—a pointy, thin nose and thin lips. He lived with his parents and two older sisters in a well-kept house with a neatly trimmed yard.

Daniel's father was an ex-marine who had grown up in this town and had returned after the service to open a machine shop with the skills he had learned in the military.

Most of his work came from local businesses, including the auto-repair shops and boatyards.

Daniel's father had a temper, and most of the town knew it. Although no one doubted that he loved his wife and his children and that he was basically a good man, he didn't seem to know how to show it. He was tough. Andrew's father used to say that someday, something would happen to Daniel's dad, and he would realize that he had wasted a lot of years being angry.

Andrew had met Daniel on the day he first moved to Telane, but since both boys were shy, it took them months to actually become friends. Daniel was an easy friend to have, as he never argued, said anything bad about anyone, or asked for things to be done his way. Whatever the others wanted was fine with Daniel. He seemed happy just to hang out with them and do what they wanted. The older boys in school often picked on Daniel and teased him about his size and quiet demeanor. Daniel never said anything back to them, which bothered Michael, who had gotten into his fair share of fights defending Daniel. Michael and Daniel never talked about this, but Daniel got even quieter and more reserved after these incidents.

Daniel was very smart—probably the smartest kid in their class. Although he never seemed to study very hard, he was a straight-A student, and he could draw better than anyone Andrew knew. Although the boys rarely went into Daniel's house, the few times they did, they were amazed by the many intricate drawings of superheroes, villains, and monsters that were stacked neatly on Daniel's desk and pinned to the walls in his room.

Andrew glanced at his watch. It was 11:52 p.m. when he and Daniel entered Michael's yard through a gap in the fence, which was well hidden beneath the long branches of a weeping willow. The two boys quickly moved along the fence until they reached the side and then the back of the garage.

From there they moved slowly through the heavy brush along the back of Michael's yard. As they neared the corner of the property, they could see Michael and William sitting on the ground, hidden from the view of anyone inside the house by two large trees.

William was the comedian in Andrew's group of friends. William was round-faced and husky. He had medium-length curly black hair and large, bright eyes; he was always talking. William could always find something funny to say, and his comedy routine often landed him in trouble with teachers.

William lived a block south of Michael in a two-story house with his two sisters and brother. William's older sister, Madison, was very smart, athletic, and attractive. Most of the boys in school had crushes on her at one time or another, especially Andrew. Madison was a little taller than Andrew, and she had long black hair that was usually pulled tightly into a ponytail. Unlike her brother, she had sharp, attractive features with green eyes and an olive complexion, a hint of the Indian heritage on her father's side. Although Andrew hadn't said anything to anyone, he really liked it when William's sister was nearby. But she was popular and a year older, and she didn't seem to notice him as anything more than just one of her brother's friends.

Madison was the only person outside of the group who had any idea of what the boys had planned to do. She had heard them talking one afternoon when she was babysitting Michael's little sister.

The boys were in the attic, and Madison could hear them talking through a vent in the ceiling. She didn't hear everything, but she did know that they had a map of Old Man Wilson's house and that there was gold in the mansion. She didn't let on to the boys that she knew anything, and they had no idea that they had been overheard. She kept a close eye on them from that day onward, waiting to see what they were going to do.

3

DISCOVERED

A few days before the boys embarked on their adventure, Madison decided to see what they were up to. Seeing all four boys sitting together and speaking quietly during lunch, Madison and her best friend, Clare, approached them.

Clare was tall and thin. She usually pulled her blond hair back in a single ponytail and wore bangs cut just above her eyebrows. The first time he had met her, Andrew thought she was a "typical girl"—always talking about clothes and boys and usually chewing gum and blowing bubbles.

"Will, don't forget you're watching Jacob and Karen tonight when Mom and Dad are out," stated Madison.

"Yeah, I know," William replied without looking at his sister and immediately returned to his conversation with the boys.

"I'm serious," scolded Madison.

"Yeah! I got it the first time," William stated firmly, looking directly at Madison. "Now, can you leave us alone, please? We're working on something."

"What?" asked Madison, sounding curious.

Sensing that William was going to say something stupid, Andrew spoke up just as William opened his mouth to reply.

"We're talking about going on a hike this weekend up Miller's Trail to check out the ghost town," Andrew said matter-of-factly.

Miller's Trail was a long hike through the coastal mountains. Everyone knew about it, but few had actually traveled it. Those who had made the six-hour hike reported that the trail ended at a small, deserted town that had been used by miners passing through from mines and campgrounds to the city of Rosemead.

Several buildings were said to be standing in the ghost town, including a saloon with a bar, tables, and chairs. As were many old remnants of the gold rush, the town was reported to be haunted. It was not a place you wanted to be stuck overnight. Perhaps this was why so few townspeople had visited the ghost town.

Given the rainstorms that were always a threat on the northern coastline, the trail could become muddy. If you were at the ghost town when the rains came, you might be stuck there for several hours, or even days, until the trail became passable again.

"Miller's Trail, huh?" replied Madison with a hint of suspicion. She looked directly at Andrew, who suddenly felt his face get warm as he realized that this was the first time he had actually spoken directly to Madison.

Madison sensed Andrew's embarrassment and hoped to get more information from him. "Why don't I believe you?" she asked.

Andrew panicked. He looked at Michael, hoping for help, but he got an equally nervous look in response.

Suddenly, Daniel blurted, "Wanna come with us?"

Madison turned to Daniel with an amused look. "With you guys?" She laughed. "I don't think so. If I wanted to hike Miller's Trail, I sure wouldn't do it with you guys. I don't want to spend the night babysitting you." With that, Madison turned abruptly and pulled Clare—who was watching the boys with a confused look on her face—by the arm.

After the girls were gone, William mimicked Daniel with sarcasm. "Do you wanna come with us?" he mocked. "Why not just hand her the map?"

"No, it was brilliant," interrupted Michael. "She stopped asking questions. You're a genius, Daniel!" Michael grabbed Daniel's shoulders and playfully shook them.

As Madison and Clare walked away, Clare asked, "Are you going to fill me in on what just happened back there?"

Madison looked over her shoulder and saw Michael and Daniel laughing. She also caught Andrew staring back at her and then quickly shifting his eyes to the floor.

Madison looked back at Clare. "They're up to something. I overheard them at Michael's house when I was babysitting. They found a map, and I think they're going to try to follow it to find some hidden gold."

"A *what*?" Clare asked in disbelief.

Madison stopped walking, faced Clare, and put her hand on Clare's shoulders as if to steady her. "Listen closely. My brother and his friends found a map of Old Man Wilson's house, and from what I can tell, it leads to some hidden gold. We're going to follow them to make sure they don't get into any trouble." Madison paused and then added, "Plus, I wouldn't mind having some money for a new car." She smiled at her best friend. "Would you?"

The following day, the four boys gathered at the public library after school to complete their research and do a final check of their facts. They wanted to be completely prepared. The boys met in a corner that was unoccupied. They spread their books over the table.

"Look at this," whispered Daniel. "It says here that the manor was built near a Native American burial ground. That's why the Wilson family didn't expand the farm fields into the woods on the south side of the property."

"My father told me about that," William said. "He said that the Native American Council has petitioned the town to buy that part of the property, but since no one can locate Old Man Wilson, they haven't been able to move forward."

"There's a reason no one goes into those woods," added Michael playfully, using his open hand to hit William lightly on top of his head. "Ghost tomahawk to the skull."

William pretended to shake and collapse as if he were dying.

"Seriously, guys. Listen to this," Daniel said. "This book says that over the past one hundred and fifty years, more than two dozen people have gone missing near those woods. People claimed to see the ghost of an Indian at night near the manor as recently as fifteen years ago!"

As Daniel read on, the boys crowded around him to get a better look at the pictures. They didn't notice Madison and Clare sneaking up and hiding behind a tall bookshelf to listen to their conversation.

"OK, enough with the ghosts," stated William. "Let's not spook ourselves outta this."

"Agreed," said Michael. "The truth is that the woods are dangerous on their own, and people get lost all the time. Let's run through the game plan for tomorrow night one more time."

As the boys began to review their plan, the girls listened intently. Once they'd heard enough, Madison whispered to Clare that it was time to go. The girls quietly made their way along the back wall of the library toward the door.

"Now let's go back and see what they have to say," said Madison.

"What for?" asked Clare.

"I just want to give them a chance to 'fess up," Madison said.

"I think you want to talk to Andrew," teased Clare.

"Don't be ridiculous. He's just a kid," replied Madison, sounding annoyed.

"Yeah, but he's a cute kid," teased Clare. She smiled coyly at Madison.

"Just shut up," said Madison. But she smiled too.

The girls approached the boys, and William was the first to see them coming.

"We got company," he stated with urgency. The boys quickly gathered their papers and closed the books.

"What's up, boys?" asked Madison.

"What do you want?" William turned, rolling his eyes.

"Researching something?" asked Clare.

"Just boring school stuff," replied William, looking down at his papers and trying to sound bored by the conversation.

"We're working on a project for history," added Daniel.

"I'm not used to seeing you so serious about homework, Will," accused Madison as her eyes darted between her brother and Andrew.

"It's a big project," Andrew blurted. Immediately, he realized that he sounded anxious, and he lowered his eyes from Madison to the floor.

"Well, you know, it's never too late to get my grades up," William said sarcastically.

"Let me see what you're working on," Madison said as she walked toward Andrew. "My C-average brother didn't just become an honor student, did he?"

Andrew quickly closed the book in front of him, and William stepped between Andrew and Madison.

"Seriously, Sis. Mind your own business," stated William more seriously.

"Fine. But I'm watching you, and you'd better not get into any trouble," Madison shot back with the same seriousness.

Madison turned and began marching away, leaving Clare facing the boys.

"Must really be a big project," Clare said with a smirk and a small shake of her shoulders. She looked at the boys and then focused on Andrew, who blushed. Clare then whipped around and followed Madison toward the exit.

4

TROUBLE IN TELANE

The day before their adventure was to begin, the boys agreed to meet in front of the school when classes ended. They were planning to go to Michael's house. "You can't be overprepared for something like this," Michael had told them earlier that day at lunch. "We need to be ready for anything."

As they walked together, chatting quietly about their plans, a police car pulled up next to them.

"Michael?" asked the police officer on the passenger side. "You're Michael Tolkin, aren't you?" he asked, pointing at Michael.

The boys all stared at Michael, who looked confused and a little frightened.

"Oh no," whispered William. "How do they know about our plan?"

"Quiet," Andrew whispered sternly.

Michael nodded his head in answer to the patrolman's question.

"We need you to come with us," the officer stated. "We have a situation with your mother."

"Is she OK?" Michael asked with a quiver in his voice.

"Yeah, yeah. She is fine, but she's in a little trouble, and we need you to come along with us so we can get this all straightened out."

Michael walked over to the officer, who was now out of his car and had opened the back door of the patrol car to let Michael in. Michael stepped into the car, but before sitting, he looked back at his friends. "I'll call you," he told them.

The patrol car sped off, leaving Andrew, Daniel, and William standing with their mouths open in disbelief.

Andrew was the first to speak. "Let's go!" he shouted as he began to run.

"Where to?" asked Daniel.

"Michael's house," Andrew responded without looking back.

The boys ran at close to full speed and reached Michael's neighborhood in ten minutes. As they neared Michael's house, they saw the patrol car parked in front. The three boys slowed down and quietly approached the front door. They were breathing heavily.

William was the last to reach the yard. "Heart attack," he whispered between heavy breaths. "I'm going to have a heart attack." He pulled his asthma inhaler from his pocket, pressed it to his lips, and took a deep breath.

"Shh," scolded Andrew, who had made his way to the window to the left of the front door.

Inside the front room of the house, the boys could see Michael and his mother and sister sitting on the couch. Across from them stood two police officers and a heavyset man in a loose, dark suit. The man was in his late forties or early fifties and had a mustache. He had combed the thin hair from the side of his head across the top to make it look like he had more hair. It wasn't working.

"What's going on?" whispered William as he finally made his way to the window.

"Not sure," answered Andrew.

"That man in the suit works at the bank," whispered Daniel. "I've seen him there when I've gone in with my dad. I think he works on all the loans."

Inside the house, the large man in the suit seemed to be getting angry. His round face was getting red, and he was raising his voice and pointing at Michael's mom.

"There is no getting around it. This is a clear-cut case of theft, and the bank and my clients want their money or the house. Simple as that," he said loudly.

"Hold on, sir, and please lower your voice," said one of the police officers. He held his hands out and made a downward motion with them. "Let's just calm down."

"Calm down? You're asking me to calm down when this woman and her family are trying to pull a fast one on the bank? This is an act of larceny, and the bank will not stand for it."

Michael's mother spoke for the first time. "Mr. Studenbaker, this is all a misunderstanding. We paid you what we owed for this month and the past-due amounts. I'm not sure what else you want."

"The checks you wrote bounced, Mrs. Tolkin, and you would have been arrested for that already if it weren't for the generosity of the police. They wanted to give you a chance to explain. But the time for explanations is over. It is obvious that you are trying to swindle the bank."

With that, Michael stood up, pointed at the banker, and growled, "You don't know what you're talking about. Why don't you shut up and stop accusing my mom?"

"Michael, that's not how we handle ourselves," scolded Mrs. Tolkin.

"Yeah, but he's full of sh—"

Before he could finish his sentence, Michael's sister put her hand over his mouth.

His mom glared at him. "Don't say another word," she hissed with her lips tight.

"I'm sorry, Mrs. Tolkin. We're going to need you to come to the station to clear this up. We understand that your daughter is eighteen, so your son can stay with her," one of the officers said quietly.

"Is she being arrested?" asked Michael's sister.

"No," responded the officer. "She just needs to come in so we can sort this out. She can call you from there if anything changes." He tried to sound comforting.

"They're coming. Let's move," stated Andrew, and the three friends quickly stood back from the window as

Michael's mom came out of the house, carrying her coat and purse. Immediately behind her was the police officer who had done all the speaking, the banker, and the other officer. Close behind them were Michael and his sister.

"I'll call you soon," Mrs. Tolkin said to her children as she reached the patrol car parked in front of her house.

As the banker left the house, he noticed the boys and glared suspiciously at them before turning toward his car, which was parked behind the patrol car.

As the patrol car pulled away, the boys walked over to Michael and his sister.

"Are you guys OK?" asked Daniel.

"I don't know," Michael's sister responded solemnly, turning to go back into the house.

The four boys stood in Michael's front yard for a while, not saying much. No one really knew what to say. They knew that it was killing Michael to see what was happening to his mom.

"Don't be late tomorrow night," Michael finally said quietly and flatly. Then he turned, walked to his front door, and went into the house, leaving Andrew, Daniel, and William standing in the front yard.

After agreeing that it was the best course of action, the three boys headed home. When Andrew got home, it was almost 4:00 p.m. He went directly to his room to make sure he had everything ready for the adventure. While he waited for his mom and dad to come home so that he could share what had happened, he worked on his homework.

Over dinner that night, Andrew told his parents about the events that had occurred at Michael's house. Andrew's mother shook her head. "That poor woman. I'm going to call to see if the kids need anything." She walked over to the phone and began searching for their number in her phone book.

Andrew's dad looked grimly back at his son. "The bank is foreclosing on a lot of properties. Seems that some outside land investors are buying up distressed properties when the owners can't pay."

"But, Dad, she said she paid them what they owed. How can they arrest her?" asked Andrew.

"I don't know, son," Dad replied. "It sounds like they were accusing her of writing bad checks. Sometimes people will do anything to protect their families. Let's hope this really is just a misunderstanding and that she can clear it all up."

"What if she can't?" asked Andrew.

"Unfortunately, they can arrest her and foreclose on the house," said his father. Then he quickly added, "But don't worry. I really don't think she did anything wrong. It's probably just a misunderstanding."

Andrew's mom, who had been talking on the phone, came back to the dinner table. "Well, there is some good news. Michael's mom is back home. She didn't say much, but she did say that she thinks this will all be resolved."

"That's good news," said Andrew's dad, sounding relieved. "There are simply too many people losing their jobs and homes in Telane." He glanced at his wife with a worried look. "We really need to think about what we'll do if one of us loses their job. We should probably start cutting back and saving a little more just in case."

Andrew listened. He'd never really thought about things like this before. He looked at his brother and sister, who were eating dinner as if without a care in the world, and then back at his parents, who were talking about some of the expenses they could cut back on, such as going out to dinner on Saturday nights. They considered selling one of their cars.

The discussion worried Andrew, and when he finished his homework later that night and went to bed, it was hard for him to fall asleep.

5

MIDNIGHT MOON

It was 11:53 p.m. on Thursday. The boys were huddled at the rear edge of Michael's yard.

"OK," said Michael in a voice that hinted of nervous energy. "Let's do a final check of supplies. Daniel, did you remember the compass?"

The compass had been a last-minute addition. Andrew had thought of it when he was watching a movie on TV. He figured that if they were underground in a tunnel or a cave, they might need it.

"Yeah, I got it," replied Daniel.

"Do you have the shovels?" asked Andrew.

"They're already down in the wash," answered Michael, referring to the dry riverbed. "All right, did everyone double-check your supplies? Flashlights, water, gloves?"

They all quickly and quietly answered yes, and without further discussion, the boys followed Michael through the missing planks in the fence and down the steep bank of the wash. When they reached the bottom of the wash, they picked up the two shovels and started north, toward the mansion.

The wash, dug hastily during the gold rush to eliminate flooding concerns, was approximately thirty yards across at the top and twenty yards across at the bottom, which made the walls steeply angled. The wash was approximately fifteen yards deep and ran through the town. It carried water from the mountains through Telane during the wet part of the year, which was October through March, with the heaviest rains in January and February. The wash started at the foot of the mountains as a large, wide-open basin. As water ran off the mountains, it was carried to the basin via many small ravines, runoffs, and shallow rivers. The basin funneled the water into the wash, which eventually emptied into the ocean in a lightly wooded area north of town.

Packed river rock formed the walls of the wash. The floor was hard-packed dirt. Brush grew haphazardly in the wash. Rocks that had tumbled from the walls or washed down from the mountains were scattered about. As the boys walked through the wash, they could feel the moist earth beneath their feet. It had rained earlier in the week, but the rain runoff had been light. There were no pools of water.

Andrew glanced at his watch; it was midnight. He felt his nervousness increasing.

As they walked quickly toward their destination, all four boys looked up at the dark clouds.

"Man, I hope it doesn't rain," said William. "I don't feel like swimming back."

6

THE WILSON MANSION

"Here it is," whispered Michael.

It sure is, thought Andrew, feeling increasingly nervous about what they were about to do.

The oak trees that surrounded the house and the pointed towers of the 150-year-old building stood tall enough for the boys to see them above the sides of the wash. One after another, they climbed the sloping rock wall until all four boys stood side by side, eyeing the once-magnificent mansion. Now it was an enormous, dark, broken-down building. The wash ran along the west side of the mansion, and from where they stood, the boys could make out the large entryway and the porch that wrapped around the front, west side, and rear of the house.

Thomas Wilson built Wilson Manor, as it was commonly called, in the mid-1800s. Thomas Wilson had three sons: Theodore, Samuel, and Thomas Jr. The Wilson family had come into a sizable sum of money during the earliest part of the gold rush of 1849, and Thomas Wilson built the manor as a hotel for the weary travelers making their way to the west coast in search of gold. Thomas was an astute businessman. He knew that the gold seekers would need services, but he also knew that the days of the gold rush would end eventually. He built the manor to serve the gold-mining customers as well as the travelers who would continue to migrate to the beautiful coastline that Telane bordered.

Upon Thomas Wilson's death, the manor's ownership was transferred to his three sons. While the Wilson family wealth and good luck lasted for the next fifty years, the family fell upon hard times in the early 1900s. Illness and accidents, including a terrible fire in the mansion, claimed many members of the family. By 1930, only a handful of the Wilsons remained. They included Daniel Wilson, who was Theodore's grandson, and John (Old Man Wilson) and Ellen Wilson, the grandson and granddaughter of Thomas Jr.

The manor, with its enormous entrance and front room, served as a hotel, a restaurant, a bar, and a dance hall. It had fifteen bedrooms, three sitting rooms, an observatory, servants' quarters, a spacious kitchen, a library, a game room, a large dining hall, and many storage rooms. All told, the manor stood three stories high and included over twenty thousand square feet of living space.

In the town library, the boys had seen pictures of the mansion in its heyday. It was a beautiful piece of architecture. Many rumors surrounded the manor. One of the most common tales was that Thomas Wilson had built his mansion over the opening to one of the most bountiful mines that he had discovered in an attempt to hide it from outsiders and claim jumpers. The rumor was that this mine *still* hid veins of gold.

Although Wilson Manor had been in Michael's family since it was built, Michael had never stepped foot in the house. Michael's father was not very close to his last surviving relatives, and Michael doubted that Old Man Wilson even knew he had relatives living in the same town.

Following Michael, the boys all crept along the west side of the building toward the back of the house. The mansion stood on over forty acres of land, most of which was behind or on the south side of the house. The land had been farmed for fruits and vegetables served in the mansion's restaurant. The fields bordered the woods, which led up to the mountains.

Entering from the front would be too risky, since anyone in a passing car would have a clear view of the building's north side. The boys quickly darted toward a towering oak tree next to the house.

"Pee break," whispered Daniel.

William looked over at him and laughed. "Nervous?" he whispered.

"Shut up," replied Daniel. "I had a lot to drink before I left the house."

And with that, the other three boys realized that they, too, had had too much to drink.

Andrew looked at his watch. It was 12:14 a.m. They were right on time. Andrew had been appointed timekeeper for the mission. It was his job to make sure they stayed on schedule. They planned to complete their mission and be back at Michael's house by 4:00 a.m. This would give them all ample time to get home, change their clothes, and crawl into bed before anyone noticed that they were gone.

Michael asked the boys to wait where they were. He disappeared around the back of the house. It was a very quiet night, except for the rustling of the trees as the October winds began to pick up. The three boys surveyed the dark building, the big oaks, and the distant tree line that marked the woods. The darkening storm clouds made the night eerie.

Suddenly, Daniel let out a quiet gasp and grabbed William's shirt.

"Something's moving over there," he said in a loud, frantic whisper. He pointed toward the front of the building.

"Where?" asked William, equally frantic, as he and Andrew scanned the dark bushes around the front of the house.

"It was over there, by the bushes," said Daniel, his voice calming down a little as he regained his composure.

"I don't see anything," said William, still trying to make out movement in the darkness.

As the three boys crouched down, staring into the darkness, Andrew felt a hand touch his shoulder.

"Whaaa!" Andrew shouted.

Someone's hand quickly covered his mouth. All three boys jumped backward and then let out simultaneous sighs of relief as they realized it was just Michael, who had returned from behind the house.

"What's wrong with you guys?" whispered Michael in an irritated tone.

"Daniel thought he saw something moving in the bushes!" William whispered anxiously.

"It was probably just a cat or something," replied Michael, his voice still hinting of irritation at their lack of courage. "Let's go. I found a way in around the back."

All three boys agreed. It was probably just a cat. They moved quickly toward the back of the house. Andrew, who brought up the rear, took a last look over his shoulder to be sure no one was there.

Their way into the house was through a window at the rear of the building. The boys crept up the back stairs of the porch and slid along the wall of the house toward the large broken window that faced the rear grounds. Rock-throwing teenagers, who would hang out drinking beer and daring their friends to enter the house, had long ago broken many of the windows. Nobody ever accepted the dare except Anthony Pedrino, who was now somewhat legendary and whose exploits only increased the mystery of the mansion.

As the story was told, Anthony, a seventeen-year-old high-school dropout who was always getting into trouble, took a dare to enter the building, climb the stairs to the third floor, and wave to his friends from an upstairs bedroom. He made his way in, and within a couple of minutes, he was leaning out of a window, waving, laughing loudly, and telling the kids below that they were a bunch of cowards. What happened next was still debated.

Fifteen minutes had passed after Anthony disappeared from the window; he hadn't come out of the building. Everyone thought he was playing a joke, and they laughed and yelled to him to be careful of that crazy Old Man Wilson.

Suddenly, the teenagers heard the sound of glass shattering, and Anthony flew out of a second-floor window, hit the porch awning, rolled off, and finally landed on the ground next to the house.

Anthony was rushed to the hospital with broken ribs, a fractured arm, and various cuts from the glass. The police report stated that Anthony had fallen out of the window in a drunken stumble, but Anthony insisted that after he had leaned out of the third-floor window, he was making his way down the stairs when he heard someone talking on the second floor. He entered the dark room, and someone pushed him to the window and then threw him out of it.

After that night, the police stepped up their patrols around the mansion. Kids stopped hanging out there, and the city council started talking about tearing the old place down. The only problem was that they couldn't locate Old Man Wilson, and he was still the legal owner of the property.

The four boys reached the open window that Michael had discovered, and Michael was the first to enter the house. He disappeared into the blackness of the room. Daniel went next, then William, and finally Andrew.

As he hiked himself up on the windowsill, Andrew glanced over his shoulder toward the rear of the yard for safety. Everything seemed a little blurry, as the autumn wind was picking up. Trees were swaying heavily, and thousands of leaves were falling through the air. Andrew took a deep breath, turned, and climbed through the window into the house.

7

INSIDE

The room they entered was dark and dusty with a strong musty odor that smelled like wet, rotting wood. Suddenly, there was light—Michael had dug into his backpack to retrieve his flashlight so that the others would do the same. The room looked as though it had been a den or a study. Old chairs were scattered around the room. Bookshelves lined the walls, and many of the books lay open on the floor with their pages turning as the wind rushed through the open window.

From a side compartment in his backpack, Michael pulled the tattered document and the maps that the boys had drawn. He cleared a space on the floor, opened the maps, and spread them out.

"According to the map, we'll have to find the kitchen to enter the basement," stated Michael.

They had been over this map a thousand times, but now that they were in the house, it seemed logical to repeat what they knew was obvious.

"The kitchen is over here, on this side," said William, pointing to a room on the map that was on the opposite side of the house from where they squatted.

With that, Michael picked up the maps and tucked them under his belt. "Let's go," he instructed, and the boys walked single file out of the study and into the main hallway of the first floor.

As they walked down the hall, they could imagine how magnificent the house had been when it was in top condition. The hallway was wide. The ceiling was high. The walls were wood-paneled about halfway up from the floor, with the upper portion covered with light-colored wallpaper decorated with small flowers and leaves. Oil lamps adorned the walls, and every few feet there were old, dusty paintings of women. In each one, the women wore long black dresses with white blouses underneath and small hats on their heads. As the boys crept silently along the hall, Andrew noticed that none of the women were smiling. That gave him the chills.

About every ten feet, there were doors on either side of the hallway. From their research, Andrew immediately recognized that these rooms must have served as the workers' quarters, since the guest rooms were all upstairs. When the manor was in its heyday, it employed upward of twenty people who served as cooks, waiters, maids, bellhops, and receptionists. Andrew and the boys had spent many hours in the town library, researching the history, structure, and layout of the house, which provided excellent details and planning tools. The manor was a big part of the town's history, and a lot had been written about it. With this information, the boys had been able to draw the interior and pinpoint their ultimate destination.

As they neared the grand entrance room at the end of the hall, the boys could feel a cool draft. The entrance room was enormous. It had a marble floor and a high ceiling. A spiral staircase led to the upstairs balcony. This room had served as the primary gathering spot for the guests. On the west side of the room was a long wooden counter that must have been a bar, and on the south side was the reception desk. The shelf behind it contained many small compartments, which probably were used to hold room keys, guests' mail, and messages.

The center of the room was sparsely furnished with a few chairs, a table, and a sofa. Opposite the entrance was a magnificent fireplace with chairs arranged in a semicircle around the opening. Above the fireplace was a large portrait of the Wilson family, including Theodore Wilson, his wife, and their three children.

As the beams of their flashlight shone like searchlights around the large room, the boys noticed that the room was very dusty. Papers and other objects were scattered across the floor. It almost looked as though someone had been looking for something and had little regard for how he left the place.

As the boys crossed the grand entranceway toward the kitchen, Andrew noticed that clumps of dirt were mixed with the dust on floor. It also appeared that there were footprints in the dust, heading in many directions.

As they reached the kitchen door, they felt a cold breeze followed by a whistling sound. They all stopped and remained very quiet.

"It's probably just the wind blowing through a broken window," said Michael.

From where they were standing, the boys could see the entire room, the grand staircase, and the balcony that led to the many bedrooms.

"Listen!" whispered Andrew.

Footsteps creaked on the floor above. At first, they were slow and soft as if someone were tiptoeing across the floor. As the boys stood frozen, listening, the footsteps sounded as if they were crossing the upstairs balcony and nearing the staircase. Andrew could feel his heart beating in his throat. His friends all stood stiffly, afraid to make a sound.

Michael looked directly at Andrew, his eyes wide. He opened his mouth as if to say something, but nothing came out.

Suddenly, there was a very loud crash upstairs. It sounded as if glass had broken or something large had fallen.

"Let's move!" William whispered loudly. Shaken, the boys ran quickly and quietly toward the kitchen door.

As they pushed through the swinging door into the kitchen, Andrew, who trailed the group, turned and looked back toward the upstairs balcony. A bright light shone upstairs. It seemed to become brighter by the second, and it was creeping toward them, illuminating the entrance room as if it were daytime.

"Something's coming!" Andrew whispered loudly as he turned away and followed the others into the kitchen.

In a panic, the boys scanned the room, searching for the basement door. It was the largest kitchen any of the boys had ever seen. In the center of the room was a long table made of metal with a wooden top, which must have served as the preparation table for meals. Above it was a rectangular metal frame about the same size as the table. The metal rectangle hung from the ceiling on chains, and hanging from it were pots and pans of various sizes. Along the walls were stoves and cabinets. To the right of the door they'd entered was a small opening in the wall, which Andrew immediately recognized as a dumbwaiter.

The dumbwaiter was a small elevator approximately two feet wide and two feet deep, operated by hand with ropes and pulleys. The staff had used it to send food from the kitchen to the upstairs floors. If a guest ordered room service, the cooks would prepare the meal, place it in the dumbwaiter, and use the ropes to pull the dumbwaiter up to the higher floor.

"Here it is!" shouted Michael, forgetting to whisper in his excitement. He pointed toward the back, in the eastern corner of the kitchen. All four boys quickly moved to the door, wondering what they would find on the other side and whether what was upstairs would be worse.

"It isn't every day that you open the basement door in a haunted house," whispered Andrew anxiously.

"It isn't every day that a ghost is chasing you, either," said William. "Just open it, already!"

The boys glanced at Andrew and then looked back at the door as Michael put his hand on the knob and began to turn it slowly.

It didn't move! It was locked! This wasn't part of the plan.

"No way!" exclaimed Michael. "We'll just have to break it down!"

"With what?" asked Daniel.

"Use the shovel to pry it open," offered Andrew. "And hurry!"

Michael took one of the shovels and placed the tip in between the door and the frame. As he pulled the handle of the shovel toward himself, the wooden door began to creak. Suddenly, there was a loud crack, and the door opened outward toward the boys.

"That was easy," said William, sounding surprised.

"The wood in this place is rotting away," replied Michael. "Let's go."

The basement steps were very steep, and the stairwell was pitch black. Michael shone his flashlight down the stairs. They could make out many wooden crates piled high on a dirt floor. The boys thought the house had smelled musty, but the damp smell that came from the basement was far worse.

"Watch yourselves. The steps may have rotted. They may not hold your weight," said Michael as he looked backed at the boys and then began to descend into the dark, cold basement of Old Man Wilson's haunted mansion.

Andrew closed the door behind them.

8

THE BASEMENTS

The old stairs creaked and popped as the boys carefully and slowly stepped into the basement. When they had all reached the dirt floor, they stood back to back, surveying the room. "Turn off your lights," instructed Michael.

The boys stood silently in the dark, listening and watching closely for any noise or light from upstairs, but there were none.

After what seemed like hours, Michael clicked his flashlight on, illuminating the faces of the other three boys who stood in a semicircle, facing him.

"Now, *that's* scary," Michael joked halfheartedly. With that, the other three boys turned on their lights and began surveying their situation.

The basement was quite large, but it had a low ceiling. Wooden crates were piled high over much of the floor. Some had been knocked over, and their contents had spilled out. The crates contained clothing, papers, canned food, old tools, and pictures. A cool draft circulated.

After a minute or so of quietly looking around the room, Michael pulled the map from his belt, opened it, and turned so that he faced the front of the house.

Daniel looked over at Michael and asked with a worried tone in his voice, "Now what do we do?"

"We have to keep going," Michael stated, not sounding completely convinced. "We can't go back. That's for sure."

"The map points to that corner," Michael whispered. The corner that he pointed to just happened to be loaded with crates.

"Great!" complained William. "We have to move all this crap."

"Looks like it," replied Andrew. The boys removed their backpacks, dropped them to the floor, and began moving crates away from the left corner of the room. They were extra careful not to make a lot of noise.

The boys worked feverishly in pairs, picking up crates and quickly piling them on the other side of the room. They were about halfway through the pile when Andrew noticed a small gap in the wall. It was near the place they were stacking the crates.

"Hold on," Andrew instructed Daniel, who was helping him. "Look, there's space along this wall that leads to the corner."

William and Michael put down their crate and rushed over to look. Andrew shone his flashlight toward the corner.

"Look!" he shouted enthusiastically.

"Shh!" the other three boys whispered in unison.

"Sorry," said Andrew, a little embarrassed.

Andrew stepped carefully along the pathway and shone his flashlight down.

"What do you see?" asked Michael.

"It's a metal hatch in the floor," replied Andrew. He pulled up on the exposed latch, and the door opened just a little. "It's the subbasement!" he whispered loudly. "And it's not locked!"

The boys stood shoulder to shoulder, shining their flashlights onto the metal hatch in the floor that led to the subbasement.

Before anyone could speak, the floor above them creaked.

"Quiet," whispered Andrew. "Do you hear that?"

The boys could hear the unmistakable sound of footsteps on the floor directly over the basement in the kitchen.

"Someone's up there," whispered Daniel.

"Or the something that was chasing us," warned Andrew.

Michael quickly moved from the corner and disappeared around the crates. Before the boys could say anything, he was already scurrying back with their backpack and shovels.

At the stairway, the door of the basement creaked open, and the boys could make out a faint glimmer of light over the crates. Michael reached down, pulled open the metal hatch, and pointed down. "Go, go, go!" he whispered frantically.

The boys quickly climbed down into the dark room below, using a cold metal ladder that was attached to the wall.

Michael was the last. As he lowered himself into the room, he reached up and pulled the door closed. They heard the distinct click of two pieces of metal latching together.

"Do you think it heard us?" Daniel asked nervously.

"I don't know, but we'd better keep moving and get out of here," replied Michael, sounding equally nervous.

With that, they lowered their eyes from the hatch door and turned their flashlights to the room around them.

The subbasement was small compared to the basement above. The walls and floor were dirt, with thick wooden beams rising from all four corners to support the ceiling. It appeared that someone had dug out this room after the construction of the manor. There was little in the room except for a few old shovels, an oil-burning lamp, a pick, and some old clothing. Several pieces of lumber leaned up against one wall.

In one corner of the subbasement, dirt was piled high, and a hole in the floor was exposed.

"The map says 'left corner, dig down,' but it looks like someone's already been here!" stated Michael.

"I knew this was a bad idea," Daniel said with real fear in his voice. "Somebody's upstairs. They've got the gold, and we're stuck in here!"

"Let's go back," added William, who also sounded concerned.

Andrew pointed his flashlight at the hatch above them.

"But how? There's no handle on this side!"

The boys stood silent for a moment, looking up to where Andrew's flashlight was pointed.

"Well, there's only one way to go, then," stated Michael, his voice surprisingly calm.

The boys moved to the corner of the subbasement and shone their lights down into darkness below them. Michael took the lead and lowered himself into the hole. Daniel went next, followed by William. Andrew was the last to go.

9

UNDERGROUND

As they lowered themselves into the room, they had to drop a few feet to the floor below, as there was no ladder to assist them this time.

Shining their flashlights up, they could see the metal hatch they'd just dropped through, swinging from hinges on the ceiling. It was obvious that this had concealed the lower room from the subbasement and that someone or something had dug the dirt away from the metal cover and opened the entrance to this room. Michael looked at the latch and then swung it closed.

"This one has a handle," he stated as he reached up and pushed the door upward, closing it with a loud click.

Michael opened the map, and all four boys moved toward the center of the room, shining their flashlights in all directions. There were tunnels dug into all four walls.

"I thought there were only supposed to be two tunnels," Andrew said.

"How are we going to know which is the right tunnel?" Daniel asked, sounding somewhat panicked.

Michael, who was reading the map, looked up and calmly instructed, "Let's split up. Everybody take a tunnel. And remember—the map says to go left, left again, left again, right, and then you should be standing in a room. If your tunnel doesn't go in those directions, come back here. If you find the right tunnel, come back and wait for the rest of us."

Daniel started to protest the idea of splitting up and then thought better of it. He did not want the other boys to think he was a coward. The tunnels were dark and damp, about four feet across and five feet high. Each of the boys picked a wall, and each started going slowly into a tunnel.

Within minutes, Daniel found the end of his tunnel. As he turned and quickly headed back toward the room, he heard the unmistakable sound of a metal latch being opened. He stopped in his tracks, leaned his back against the tunnel wall, and turned off his flashlight.

Michael had just made his second left turn when he heard the metal latch opening up. He also turned off his flashlight and stopped to listen.

Andrew made one left turn and was traveling along a straightaway course that seemed to go downhill. He could feel the ground becoming increasingly moist under his feet as his shoes sank ever so slightly into the earth. He heard the metal sound and stopped. He listened but could only hear the sound of his own breathing. He thought for a moment and continued walking.

William had made two lefts and could see another left turn approaching. "This must be the right tunnel," he said to himself as he turned the corner and shone his flashlight forward.

Suddenly, William screamed. He stood face-to-face with a human skeleton! William stepped backward, tripped over his own feet, and fell onto his back, still shining the flashlight at the standing skeleton. William gasped, but the skeleton did not move.

When he realized that the skeleton wasn't coming toward him, William got up and moved toward the bones. He could now see that the skeleton had shreds of clothing left on it. A large knife was stuck through its ribs, and this had kept the skeleton pinned to the wall where the tunnel ended. William started walking backward with his light still on the skeleton. He then turned and quickly headed back through the tunnel to the center room.

Daniel could make out a faint light and shadows of movement from his position within the tunnel. There was definitely someone or something moving about in the room where the boys had split up to explore the individual tunnels. He heard a scream, and the shadows quickly disappeared. He slowly crept forward along the side of the cave, trying to get a better look and hoping to rejoin his friends.

Michael, who hadn't left his spot in his tunnel, also heard the scream. It sounded like William. Michael moved quickly toward the center room.

Michael was the first to enter the room. He moved to the tunnel that William had taken and stood in the entrance.

"William?" he called in a loud whisper.

"Michael?" came a faint response from behind him. Michael, startled, turned around quickly. Daniel emerged from his tunnel, his flashlight still off.

"Did you hear the latch open?" asked Daniel. "And the scream?"

"Yeah," responded Michael. He shone his flashlight up. The metal door in the ceiling was now wide open.

Daniel and Michael turned back toward William's tunnel. They could hear his heavy breathing as he approached the room. Before the boys could ask, William, out of breath, told them about the skeleton. "I turned a corner, and there was a skeleton, knife in the gut, stuck up against a wall. Scared the crap out of me!"

"We thought you ran into whoever opened the latch from the subbasement," Daniel said.

"The whoever that opened the what?" asked Michael, concerned.

Andrew suddenly appeared in his tunnel opening. "I found it!" he whispered.

"Then let's get out of here," stated William, and all four boys quickly headed into Andrew's tunnel.

Andrew's tunnel had continued on a downward slope toward the room that was their mapped destination. As the boys made their way through the tunnel, they felt dampness not only on the floor but also on the walls and in the air.

The boys made the final right turn and slowly entered the room. The room was very small and had a low ceiling. Wooden pillars in all four corners supported the beams that held up the ceiling. All four boys moved toward the center of the room and shone their flashlights toward the ceiling.

"All I see is dirt," Daniel said with a hint of worry in his voice.

"That's 'cause we're surrounded by it," William responded.

The boys searched the ceiling with their flashlights and could find nothing that helped them to make sense of the last instruction on the map: "Look up and use your imagination."

Andrew reached up and brushed the ceiling with his hands, causing dirt and dust to fill the air. As he continued to brush away dirt, the boys could see that he was uncovering something. Soon, all four boys were brushing the ceiling with their hands. Dirt fell on their faces, and the dust became almost too thick to see through. They started to cough.

"Look!" shouted Michael, between coughs, shining his flashlight at the ceiling. "It's a drawing. A map."

The low ceiling was covered from corner to corner with the drawing of an elaborate maze of tunnels and rooms. Like the boys' map, this one had the same four designs in each corner. The map was painted with light colors and had been sealed with some type of glossy coating to ensure that it wouldn't simply brush off or seep into the dirt. It was very clear. Arrows pointed from the left of the map to the right. A large X was painted over the word "GOLD."

"The map shows that our tunnel should continue through the room," said Andrew as he walked to the right side of the room and began brushing and then scraping the dirt on the wall with the back of his flashlight.

Within seconds, the dirt gave way to a doorway!

Daniel quickly opened his backpack and pulled out a pencil. "Here. Let me have the map," he said, pulling the parchment from Michael's hands. He placed the map on the floor, looked up at the ceiling, and then began copying that map on the blank side of their paper map.

Daniel completed the map, while Michael and William worked together to pull open the old wooden door that Andrew had uncovered.

The door creaked open, exposing a small tunnel with barely enough room for one boy at a time to fit through. The tunnel smelled of old, stale, damp air. It was also very cold and covered with old spider webs.

"OK, who will go first?" asked William in a tone that indicated that he definitely was not volunteering.

"I'll go," answered Michael, not exactly sounding sure of himself either. Michael entered the small tunnel, and the boys followed in single file.

Andrew shone his flashlight onto his wrist. It was 1:45 a.m. They were still on schedule.

The map on the ceiling had shown a maze of tunnels that would confuse anyone who wasn't lucky enough to have a copy. With the map in their possession, the path seemed very clear to the boys. After a few minutes of slowly creeping through the tunnel, they exited into a larger hallway of sorts with several tunnels on either side.

They entered the hallway, and Andrew suggested taking a short break. Each boy dropped to a squat in the hallway and opened his backpack to take a drink from his water bottle.

After a quick drink, Michael surveyed the map that Daniel had drawn.

"This way," he stated, looking down at the map and then pointing into the second small opening on the left side of the hallway. "Ready?"

The boys all stood up silently, gathered their backpacks, and went deeper into the maze of tunnels.

As they moved single file through the tiny tunnel, Andrew, who was last, whispered, "Wait...listen."

Behind them in the tunnel, they could hear the sound of footsteps. The boys stood frozen. They could make out a beam of light. The footsteps sounded like someone was running.

"Let's get out of here!" shouted William frantically, and the boys began moving as fast as they could through the tunnel.

As they ran, they could hear noises behind them. It sounded as if someone was shouting at them, and that made the boys run even faster. As they pushed forward, Michael could make out a small opening ahead of them.

"Hurry!" he shouted.

Just then, William's foot caught Michael's heel and tipped him headlong in the tunnel. All three boys crashed into him and sprawled into a small room within the tunnel.

As all the boys lay on the ground, trying to untangle themselves, a bright light shone on them from the tunnel. They all looked toward the light. It blinded them, preventing them from being able to see anything else.

"Don't kill us! We're just kids!" William pleaded.

"Don't kill you?" responded a familiar voice. "I won't kill you, but I can't guarantee that Mom won't. We've been trying to catch up to you since the basement."

The flashlight that shone in their eyes turned to the ground, and the boys could see the predator. It was Madison, and directly behind her was Clare!

10

AND TWO MAKES SIX

"What the heck are you doing here?" William demanded of his sister.

"I've been following you. I knew you boneheads would get into trouble. Besides, I found out earlier tonight that those two men who were in the hardware store six months ago buying digging equipment were spotted again yesterday—this time, in the hills behind this house," stated Madison in an all-knowing voice.

"The Indian burial ground," said Daniel quietly.

"How did you know what we were doing?" asked Andrew.

"I heard you talking up in Michael's attic one day when I was there babysitting, and I saw what you were doing in the library. When I heard William sneaking out of the house, I texted Clare, telling her to meet me here," replied Madison.

"By the way, it was faster just riding our bikes here. We had to wait for you guys to crawl up out of the wash," Clare said in a know-it-all tone.

Andrew felt a little embarrassed. Maybe they had over-thought some of their plan.

"So you made the footsteps we heard and shone the light we kept seeing behind us?" Andrew asked.

"We came in the front door and hid upstairs by the balcony, waiting for you guys," responded Madison, sounding almost excited. "When we saw you coming across the entrance room, we followed." She paused for a second, looking from Andrew to the rest of the group. "Now, where do we go?"

Michael, who looked irritated, stated, "Well, William, you gotta split your share with your sister and Clare. Let's keep moving."

Andrew looked at the three other boys; they didn't appear happy that Madison and Clare were joining them.

Funny thing, Andrew thought. I really don't mind that they are here.

After dusting themselves off and picking up their gear, the boys once again began moving.

They passed a few open caverns that looked like naturally formed rooms and continued to follow the map, which led them to a very long, narrow tunnel that seemed to go on forever. They walked in a single line with Michael first, followed by William, Daniel, Clare, Madison, and Andrew. Andrew didn't particularly like being in small places. This tunnel was making him anxious, as it was the smallest tunnel that they had been in yet. He was happy that he was last so that no one else would see his growing concern—especially Madison.

"Do you see the end yet?" he asked.

"You don't need to keep asking that," Madison said softly, glancing over her shoulder. "That's like the fifth time in the last two minutes." She smiled faintly.

"Yeah, I think so," replied Michael from the front.

The tunnel began to narrow even more. They had to swat crawl and then finally crawl on their hands and knees to continue.

In the distance, the group could hear a faint rustling sound.

Michael stopped. "Hold on!"

"What is it?" asked William.

Michael didn't respond.

"Michael, what do you see?" asked Daniel.

"A river," Michael replied in amazement.

"A what?" asked William.

"It's an underground river," said Michael, still sounding amazed.

One by one, the children lowered themselves out of the small tunnel and onto the west bank of the river about five feet below, the person exiting the tunnel turning to help the next in line. Once they were all out, they stood quietly, amazed at the natural wonder of the cave.

The cave chamber was enormous. Through the center of the chamber ran a slow-moving river with muddy banks on each side. The chamber was about twenty yards across and at least fifteen yards tall from the surface of the river to the ceiling. The water came from under the north wall of the cave and traveled south for as far as the eye could see, but it appeared to narrow the further south it moved. From their vantage point, they couldn't see where the cavern ended.

Daniel, standing directly behind Michael, said, "This definitely isn't on the map." He pulled the map from the back of Michael's backpack where it was tucked.

"Let me see it," demanded Michael. "This was the X, but where is the gold?" he asked, pointing to the map and then looking at the cavern.

Andrew and William looked south and then at each other.

"What do you think?" William asked softly.

Andrew turned and replied, "I'm not sure. If we follow the cave, we might never make it out of here. And if we don't—"

"The gold could be just around the corner," interrupted Michael, finishing Andrew's sentence as he folded the map and handed it back to Daniel.

Andrew looked at his watch. It was 2:30 a.m. They had planned to have found the gold by now, loaded it into their bags, and started for home. Instead, they were looking at yet another setback.

"What do we do?" asked Andrew, now speaking loud enough for everyone to hear. "If we go forward, we'll be running late."

"Late for what?" asked Madison.

"We planned to get back home by 4:00 a.m. to be sure our parents wouldn't suspect anything," replied Andrew quietly.

"We'll, we've come this far. We might as well go a little farther. At least until we see where this river goes," Michael said in a half-encouraging, half-pleading tone.

"He's right," stated Madison.

Andrew look surprised that Madison had agreed.

"What's the point of getting this close and giving up? If you leave now, you'll just want to come back again. Might as well take this to the end, and if you find the gold, then great. If not, so be it. At least you tried," Madison concluded.

"Oh, sounds like a great idea," Clare said sarcastically.

"Then let's do this," said Andrew as he looked directly at Madison.

That was that; they were going to continue.

The group moved south along the west bank until it narrowed and disappeared, making it unsuitable for walking. The group waded across the knee-high river to the east bank. As they moved along, they began to hear faint clicking sounds in the distance. They stopped occasionally to listen, but the sounds seemed very far off, and no one had any idea what they might be.

As they continued south, the cave got narrower. "It's not much farther," encouraged Michael.

Michael led the group, followed closely by William and Daniel. Andrew walked directly behind them, with Clare and Madison trailing by a few feet. As they walked, Madison quickened her pace to be side by side with Andrew.

"So what happens when we find the gold?" she asked.

"We pack what we can carry in our backpacks and go back the way we came," Andrew responded.

"Not that," Madison said. "I mean what happens when people find out about this place? It's not like we'll be able to keep it a secret for long—especially when we start spending money."

"I don't know," Andrew said, pausing. "I guess we really didn't think about that. For me, it was more about the adventure and helping Michael than having the gold for myself. This means a lot to him…for his family."

"You're a good friend," Madison said, putting her hand on Andrew's shoulder.

Andrew smiled at Madison, who blushed a little and smiled back.

They neared the end of the cavern, and Michael began jogging ahead of the group.

Suddenly Michael shouted, "No!" He sounded very disappointed.

Directly in front of them, the cavern simply ended abruptly at a wall of dirt and rock. The river continued on, moving under the wall.

"I guess this is the end of the road," said William, sounding defeated, as the group caught up with Michael.

"All this for nothing," added Daniel dejectedly.

"Well, at least you tried," said Madison, but she sounded disappointed too.

"Anyway, the water level seems to be rising, and it's probably a good idea to head back," said Clare, surveying the river and looking very worried.

Michael, who was in the front, just stood still with his back to the others. He said nothing. Andrew knew that this adventure had meant more to Michael than to the others. It was Michael's map, and the owner of the mansion had been his relative. Most of all, he had wanted to find the gold so that he could fill the void left by his father, fix up his house, and take care of his mother, who worked so many hours and always looked so tired.

"We'd better start back," said Andrew, putting his hand on Michael's shoulder.

Michael still said nothing. He just stood quietly, watching the water run under the rock wall.

The group turned and slowly started back. Nobody said a word. After a few feet, Andrew turned back to Michael. "Maybe we could come back another time and…" His voice trailed off as Michael stripped off his backpack and stepped into the river.

"Michael, wait!" shouted Andrew, but it was too late.

Michael lowered his body into the river and disappeared into the murky water directly in front of the cavern wall.

Andrew removed his backpack and waded into the river, searching for Michael with his arms and hands. The river was level with Andrew's chest and seemed to be moving quicker than it did when they had first caught a glimpse of it earlier.

"He must have gone under the wall!" shouted Andrew.

"Don't try it!" shouted Madison, realizing that Andrew might be thinking about following Michael under the wall.

Andrew felt around for Michael again and then slowly moved out of the water and back onto the bank.

"What do you think is over there?" asked Daniel.

"Some air, I hope," answered William.

"Now what do we do?" asked Clare, sounding panicky.

At that very moment, the water began to ripple. Bubbles rose to the surface, and Michael's head appeared.

"It's incredible!" he shouted excitedly. Water ran from his hair over his face. "You have to see this!"

"What is it?" asked Madison anxiously.

"Gold!" shouted Michael. "Bring your packs and follow me!" And with that, he dove back under the water, under the rock wall, and disappeared.

The others looked at each other with a mixture of awe and confusion. Andrew was the first to react. He smiled at Madison and pulled off his backpack to carry it in his hands. "What are we waiting for?" he said as he waded in and then dove into the water.

Madison pulled her backpack off and started into the water.

"Seriously?" asked Clare as Madison shrugged and disappeared into the water. She turned to see Daniel and William too removing their backpacks and entering the water.

11

GOLD!

They splashed to the surface one by one, waded to the bank, and stood still in the cold, ankle-deep water, overwhelmed by the sight before them. They had entered a cavern the size of a football stadium. The cavern walls rose upward sharply, and a faint, dusty light shone in from above, illuminating the cavern with an eerie glow. The walls of the cavern appeared to be primarily rock, with streams of dark gold branching in many directions. Michael was already out of the water and standing on the shore, facing the group. He reached down to the sandy earth that covered the cavern floor and picked up a marble-sized rock.

"It's gold!" Michael said, brimming with enthusiasm. "I knew we'd find it! I knew it was here!"

The others waded out of the water and ran in all directions, picking up the small gold nuggets that lay scattered over the cavern floor. They gathered all they could carry, ran back to the river edge, dropped the gold in a pile, and then ran back to the cavern to collect more. Finally, after half an hour of running, they collapsed, excited and exhausted by what was now a two-foot-high pile of gold nuggets.

"I think we're rich," stated Daniel.

"No, we are *very* rich!" replied William as they all began to laugh and talk excitedly about their find.

"I'm going to buy myself an ice-cream shop," William said, laughing. He tossed a nugget into the air, caught it, and then tossed it again.

"I'm going to get a car," Madison chimed in.

"All new clothes for me," added Clare.

Andrew stood up and walked over to Michael, who was standing behind the others, looking at the opening in the top of the cavern, where the moonlight was shining through.

"We did it," said Andrew softly. "I know how important this was to you."

"Yeah," Michael replied softly. "I can't believe we actually found it."

Andrew looked down at the watch on his wrist. It was 3:23 a.m. He put his hand on Michael's shoulder. "We gotta go."

Andrew turned and walked back to the others, who were still laughing and talking about how they were going to spend their fortune.

"I hate to break up the party, but we'd better get out of here," he said. "We're running way behind."

"Let's load up the gold and get back," stated Michael, joining the group. He smiled broadly and felt a sense of victory.

They all worked quickly, picking up the gold and loading it into their backpacks. The gold was much heavier than they expected, and they were only able to pick up half of what they had gathered.

"I guess this will still make us all rich," said William, who looked somewhat disappointed that they couldn't carry it all.

"Who says we can't come back for it some other time?" asked Madison. "We're the only ones who know that it's here," she finished with a smile.

Andrew picked up his backpack, swung it over his shoulder, and stepped into the river.

"Hey!" he exclaimed. "The water's rising!"

Sure enough, the water level seemed to have risen at least a foot.

"And it looks like the water is moving quicker," added William.

"It's the rain," said Madison, sounding as if she should have figured it out earlier. "It must be raining awfully hard outside, and the river is carrying the rainwater from the mountains to the ocean."

"This might be why the gold is on the floor. This cavern probably floods, causing the walls to give up some of the rocks and gold," added Andrew.

"Let's move," commanded Michael.

With that, they all entered the cold water with a renewed sense of urgency and pulled their heavy backpacks under the water and back to the other side of the cavern wall.

When they reached the other side, it was apparent that the water level had risen dramatically. The sandy bank of the river where they had watched Michael dive in was now under water.

"We have to get over to the other side!" yelled Andrew as he helped the rest of the group out of the water, not realizing that he had raised his voice to be heard over the fast-moving water.

"Stay close to the side where the water is shallow," responded Madison.

They moved upstream until they reached the very wet and muddy bank in the small room under the tunnel. One by one, they climbed into the dark tunnel with their backpacks heavy with gold.

They slowly made their way back through the maze, stumbling and bumping into one another. Only Daniel's flashlight had survived the underwater trip, and its light was barely strong enough to illuminate a few yards ahead in the tunnels.

"Waterproof gear next time," noted William.

When they reached the hallway with the many tunnels, Michael turned and asked Daniel for the map. Daniel's face suddenly turned pale as he searched his pockets.

"Don't tell us you lost it," said William in a joking tone as he tried to sound unconcerned.

"It's gotta be here," replied Daniel, dropping to his knees to search his backpack. "I know it is." He suddenly stopped looking. "I must have lost it in the river," he said with his head down.

"Great!" said William. "Now what are we going to do?"

"It's long gone now," stated Michael.

"Well, does anyone remember which tunnel we came out of?" asked Andrew, looking down the large hallway at the many tunnel openings.

"I remember that it was pretty close to the tunnel we just came out of," stated Daniel, hoping to make amends for losing the map.

"He's right," said Michael.

"Then it must be one of these tunnels," added Andrew, pointing across the dirt floor toward three tunnel openings.

"Should we split up?" asked Michael, sounding unsure of himself.

"We only have one flashlight," replied Andrew.

"Andrew's right," Madison said. "We'd better stay together."

Andrew turned and looked over at Madison, feeling himself blush. He felt good that Madison agreed with him, but her confidence in his statement had embarrassed him.

"Well, pick a tunnel. Any tunnel," joked William.

"I think it was this one," said Michael, still not sounding completely sure.

"Then we might as well give it a shot," responded Andrew.

And with that, the group headed into the darkness of the tunnel, not sure where they would end up.

They had been in the tunnel for what seemed like an hour but was really only fifteen minutes, according to Andrew's watch, when they first heard the sound.

Click, click.

The sound was faint, and Andrew was the first to hear it. "Stop! Listen!" he whispered to the others. "Do you hear that?"

Click, click. The sound went again.

"It sounds like it's coming from up ahead," whispered Michael.

They continued walking, and the sound grew louder and louder. It turned from a faint click to a loud clank of metal hitting stone.

12

NOT ALONE

The tunnel opened into a larger cave about ten feet high and ten feet across. It seemed as though the noise was directly ahead of them, and the group could see light illuminating the cave in the direction of the sound. "This wasn't the right tunnel," whispered Michael.

"Let's go back," Daniel said frantically. "Before whatever's over there sees us."

"Let's go!" added Michael as he turned back, only to run directly into the chest of a very large, very mean-looking man.

"Ahhhh!" screamed Michael at the top of his lungs as the enormous man grabbed him by the arm and, in another swift move, grabbed William by the neck. William could only manage to grunt.

The others screamed and ran in different directions. Andrew scurried behind the large man and back into the tunnel from which they'd come. Daniel headed toward the darkness of the large cave. Madison, followed by Clare, ran toward the light. Suddenly, she was face-to-face with another man who was pointing a shotgun directly at her.

"You better slow down," he bellowed.

Madison stopped running. Clare slammed into her from behind with a loud *oomph* and then they both stood very still, staring directly at the barrel of the shotgun. The large man easily pulled Michael and William across the cave and threw them to the floor by Madison and Clare's feet.

"What are you doing here?" he shouted angrily.

The large man was at least six foot five, as he had to hunch over to keep from hitting his head on the ceiling of the cave. He was muscular and stocky, making him even more formidable. He was wearing dark jeans and a dark flannel shirt with the sleeves rolled up to his elbows, showing off several circular, black tattoos on his forearms. His face was weathered, indicating that he spent a good deal of time outdoors, and the scar tissue around his eyes and the crooked nose suggested that he'd been in many fights in his lifetime. He wore a faded New York Yankees baseball cap over thick, dark hair. The slight accent evident in his deep, booming voice also suggested that he was from the East Coast.

"We...we were just looking around," stammered Michael.

"Looking for what?" asked the man with the shotgun.

This man was the opposite of the large man. He was shorter, probably five foot seven, and overweight, which gave him a very round appearance. He also wore dark jeans. His black T-shirt seemed a little too small for him and showed off his belly as he raised his arms to point the shotgun. He face was unshaven and round, and his voice was low and rough. It was the voice of someone who had smoked cigarettes all his life. He was balding; hair circled the back of his head. The bandana around his neck looked like it was used to catch the sweat that was beading up on his face.

"Nothing," answered Michael, gaining his composure. "We just wanted to explore the house."

"And you just happened to find your way down into the caves, eh? Don't lie to me, boy, or I'll break your neck!" the large man said as he stepped aggressively toward William.

He pulled William to his feet, opened his backpack, and reached in to remove a nugget of gold. The large man's eyes grew wide, and his mouth opened.

"It's gold," he said to the other man, sounding as if he didn't believe it. "They found the gold!"

"Where did you find it?" shouted the man with the shotgun, pointing it directly at William. William looked at the man and then quickly glanced toward Michael.

"Tell me where, or you'll die right here," the man continued. He swung around and aimed the shotgun at Michael. "I guess you're the leader," he said accusingly.

Michael stood silently and stared back at the man with the shotgun.

"I won't tell you again, boy!" the man bellowed.

Michael said nothing. He just stared back at the man.

The man's grip tightened on the shotgun, and his finger began to move to the trigger.

"Wait!" yelled William. "We found it by the underground river. It's back down that cave."

"There ain't nothing down that cave except a lot of dirt and more caves, most of which end in a pit that you'd never be able to crawl out of," replied the large man.

"Now, where did the gold come from?" he demanded. "And I won't ask you again!"

"He's telling you the truth," begged Madison. "Back through that tunnel is the room with all the tunnel openings. The tunnel straight across leads to the gold."

"How was it that you happened to know exactly what tunnel to take?" the large man asked suspiciously.

"We had a map," Michael said, figuring that lying would do no good.

"Well, then, hand it over," demanded the man with the shotgun.

"It's lost. We lost it when we were crossing the river," replied Michael.

"I told you not to lie to us," roared the large man, reaching down toward Michael. He grabbed him by the arm and pulled him to his feet.

"He's not lying!" yelled Madison, becoming frightened. "You can search our things…We lost it." Madison lowered her voice as she finished her sentence.

As the man with the shotgun stood guard, the large man grabbed their backpacks and searched them, amazed at the amount of gold they contained. But he did not find a map.

"Joe, over here," the man with the shotgun motioned to the large man.

The two men backed away from the group and began whispering to one another, keeping the shotgun aimed directly at Michael. As they spoke, Michael was able to get a better view of their surroundings.

They were at the end of the cave, and it appeared that the men had been mining it. One wall seemed freshly picked away. Michael figured that they had been looking for the gold. They must be the men that the newspaper reporter had written about. Scattered around the floor were tools, lanterns, and supplies. The walls in this part of the cave appeared to be some sort of rock, but Michael saw no trace of gold.

Daniel could feel the tears welling up in his eyes as he ran into the darkness of the cave. He had run into walls and tripped over rocks, but he continued to move through the darkness. Finally, he stumbled over a large pile of rock and fell headlong to the ground. He listened, but he didn't hear footsteps. He could only hear his own heavy breathing. He pulled himself over to the side of the cave and lay there, trying to catch his breath. He was very afraid. He began to cry quietly.

Andrew moved through the tunnel slowly, using his hands to guide him through the darkness, and within minutes, he reached its end. As his eyes adjusted to the heavy darkness, Andrew could barely make out another opening and tunnel to his right. He turned and listened but heard nothing. Andrew couldn't keep his thoughts straight as they raced through his mind.

"What am I going to do?" he asked himself. "Should I try the other tunnel and see if I can find my way out? Should I go back and try to help my friends?"

"OK, on your feet!" ordered the man named Joe.

Michael, Madison, Clare, and William stood and faced the man.

"You're gonna take us back to that gold," Joe ordered.

"And you better not play any games with us, or we'll kill you right here and leave you to the rats and spiders," added the other man.

With that, the two men motioned for Madison, Clare, and the two boys to lead them back to the large cavern with the gold. They moved slowly through the tunnel, with Joe leading the way. The man with the shotgun followed behind to make sure that nobody tried to get away. Eventually, they reached the hallway of tunnels and stood in the middle of the room, trying to remember which tunnel would lead them back to the gold.

"This is it," stated Michael.

"It better be," hissed the large man.

"You go first." Joe motioned to Madison. "If this is the wrong tunnel, then you'll be the first to die."

Clare looked at Madison, her face dirty with lines from her tears. Madison looked at her and whispered encouragement as she slowly entered the cave, followed by Joe, Clare, William, Michael, and the man with the gun.

"Tate," barked Joe, "keep a close eye on those two." He pointed at the boys. "I don't want them getting any bright ideas about getting away."

Michael knew that it was hopeless to try to escape now. His only hope would be once they had reached the large cavern. He remembered seeing caves exiting the cavern on the north side while he was collecting gold. Once the men found the gold, they would be preoccupied, and maybe he and the group could make a run for the tunnels. He only hoped those tunnels would lead to safety.

Andrew decided to try to go back to help his friends. He started back into the tunnel when he heard voices echoing through it.

He stepped backward, lowered himself to the floor, and listened. He heard Michael's voice and then the voices of the two men. He knew they were going back for the gold.

He waited a couple of minutes to be sure they were gone and began to backtrack toward the hallway when suddenly the ground gave way below him, and he fell backward into a hole, landing with a thud. Dirt and gravel fell down on top of him. Andrew lay back, trying to catch his breath, as the fall had knocked the wind out of him. Dust was everywhere, and he couldn't see a thing as he gasped for air.

He took small breaths until he recovered, and it took a minute for the dust to settle. When it did, he realized that he was in a large pit. The pit was too deep to crawl out of.

It's a trap, he thought, and I'm stuck.

Andrew lay in the pit, trying to figure out what to do. He decided to wait for a few minutes, hoping that the men and his friends would make it into the large cavern. Then he would call out in hopes that Daniel would hear him—if he were still around and hadn't been captured.

Andrew was feeling truly scared for the first time that evening. What if he was never found? What if he didn't see his family again?

As he lay in the pit, Andrew's thoughts turned to his brother and sister.

Anna, who was nine, had long black hair like his mother's and a slender face and bright eyes. She was an outgoing, friendly girl whom Andrew admired. She didn't seem to let anything get to her. Andrew and his sister got along very well.

On the other hand, Andrew's little brother, Erik, who was four, was an accident waiting to happen. Full of spirit and with a knack for breaking things, he was as thick and solid as a tractor. He had a mound of messy, dark-brown hair and a round face. Erik moved nonstop and at full speed 100 percent of the time until he laid his head on the pillow, and then he was out like a light, snoring like a bear. Even the loudest noises failed to disturb his sleep.

Andrew had nicknamed his brother "the tornado." If you were in his path, watch out; Erik left a swath of destruction behind him.

Andrew's thoughts were interrupted by a faint glimmer of light above him that appeared to be growing brighter. It seemed to be coming in the direction of his tunnel. The light glowed and increased in intensity just like the light he had seen in the mansion earlier when he and the boys were looking for the basement. The light grew very bright, so bright that Andrew had to cover his eyes.

Suddenly, the light was gone. Andrew screamed as a large hand grabbed his wrist, pulled him upward out of the pit, and dropped him onto the tunnel floor.

"There're a lot of traps in this old mine," stated a voice calmly and matter-of-factly.

Andrew's eyes adjusted from the brightness back to the dark, and he could make out a very large man's figure. The man wore jeans and a flannel shirt. His heavy, brown work boots were covered in dried mud. Andrew moved closer and could see that the man was very old, although his frame was large and strong. His skin was leathery and wrinkled, showing his age and indicating that he had spent a lot of time outdoors. Andrew also noticed that he looked somewhat familiar. His pale eyes had a kind appearance, in sharp contrast to his large, intimidating size.

"Who are you?" asked Andrew.

"A friend," replied the man.

With that, the man turned and walked away swiftly. Andrew followed, almost jogging just to keep up. Andrew looked at the man from head to toe as he followed. Something's not right, he thought.

13

FEAR

Daniel pushed himself up with his hands and stood in the complete darkness. It seemed as though he had run deep within the cave. He was no longer sure which direction he had come from. Daniel had carried the flashlight as he ran. He must have dropped it when he fell. He got down on his knees and began to search for the flashlight with his hands. After a few minutes, Daniel's hand brushed the cool metal of the flashlight. He shook it, and a faint glimmer of light shone through the darkness to the wall of the cave.

Daniel pointed the flashlight in different directions. I think I came this way, he thought. With that, he began moving south in the tunnel, away from the direction from which he had come.

Michael, Madison, Clare, William, and the two men entered the natural cavern that the river ran through. The river was now moving much faster, and the water level had certainly risen. They lowered themselves onto the bank and began to walk toward the south end of the cavern.

After the fifteen-minute walk, the group stood at the cavern's end. "It's under the cavern wall," Michael said. "We swam in the river, and under the wall is another cavern with the gold." Michael motioned with his hand toward the river.

"You've got to be kidding," accused Tate.

"I told you not to lie to me, boy," grunted Joe, grabbing Michael by his sweatshirt.

"I...I...told you! It's under the wall. Why would I lie to you?" Michael stammered, frightened by Tate's aggressiveness.

Tate moved close to Joe and whispered, "You know I can't swim, Joe."

Joe looked angry. "Well, damn!" he shouted. "You stay here with them, and I'll check the other side," he said to Tate. Then turning his attention to Michael, Madison, Clare, and William, he said, "And if you're lying to me, you all die right here."

He stated those last words with such conviction that the four knew that he was serious. Joe put his lantern down on the ground and walked slowly into the river.

The river moved quickly, and Joe seemed to be having a difficult time standing up. The water level appeared to be rising with every second. Finally, Joe reached the wall and disappeared under water and toward the gold.

Daniel moved slowly through the tunnels, following the faint glimmer of his flashlight. He followed the tunnel he thought was the one the group had turned down earlier, but now he wasn't sure he had gone in the right direction.

After a few minutes, he came to a fork in the tunnel and realized he had gone in the wrong direction. This was not the tunnel that led to the cavern. He was lost.

Daniel turned off his flashlight and began to weep quietly. He cursed himself for feeling so timid and always being afraid. He wondered why he couldn't be more like his friends, like the son his father really seemed to want. His father would never say it, but Daniel knew that he was a disappointment to him. Daniel's father had been a star athlete in school and very popular, even dating a cheerleader. Daniel couldn't even muster the courage to ask a girl a simple question, let alone ask a girl out. Daniel didn't take risks. He wasn't great at sports. He was conservative and thoughtful in everything he did, and he was painfully shy. Sometimes at night, when he couldn't sleep, Daniel wondered why his friends even hung out with him.

After several minutes of sitting in the dark quietly, Daniel switched on his flashlight and directed the beam at the wall in front of him. As his flashlight flickered, he noticed drawings on the wall. He stood up to look closer and realized that the pictures looked very much like images attributed to the early Native American tribes who lived in the area. He'd seen those pictures in books at the library.

Daniel walked slowly along the cave wall, following the images. They seemed to tell the story of a young Indian boy who was hunting a great bear. The bear had attacked and injured several members of the boy's tribe, and he ventured out into the forest on his own to find the bear before it could come back to hurt anyone else.

As the story unfolded in pictures, Daniel began to gain courage. The images on the wall began to talk to him. He started to feel that they were intended for him. The last set of drawings showed the young Indian boy finding the bear, slaying it, and returning to his tribe with the news of his victory.

Daniel's hand touched the final image of the boy, who had now become a man and wore the headdress of the tribal leader.

Determined, Daniel began to make his way forward, deeper into the tunnel.

Andrew was worried. What if this was one of the men from the group that had grabbed his friends? What if he was just leading him to the others? The old man moved quickly, but Andrew was slowing down as his suspicions grew. Finally, he stopped dead in his tracks. The old man was almost out of Andrew's sight when he turned back and looked at Andrew.

"Do you want to get out of here or not?" asked the old man.

Without waiting for an answer, he simply turned around and continued to walk. Andrew unstuck his feet from the floor and quickly followed the man, realizing that his options were limited. It seemed that he was just going to have to trust the old man.

The old man didn't say another word. He just moved through the tunnels with Andrew a few yards behind. Andrew didn't speak, either. He was afraid. At the same time, he was thankful that the man had found and helped him. The man then stopped at an intersection with another tunnel. He turned to Andrew and said, "If you follow this tunnel, you'll find your friends." He pointed to one tunnel entrance.

"And if you follow this one," he said, pointing in the opposite direction, "you'll find what you came for and a way out."

"Take this," added the man, holding his lantern out to Andrew, who cautiously took it.

When the man handed over the lantern, the light shone directly into Andrew's eyes, causing him to shield his eyes with the back of his hand. When the bright light subsided, he lowered his hand, and as his eyes adjusted to the darkness again, he realized the old man was gone.

Daniel continued to crawl through the twisting, turning tunnel for almost twenty minutes. Just as he was beginning to get discouraged, he heard the faint sound of voices somewhere up ahead.

Daniel moved toward the voices and then, just ahead, he saw a faint glimmer of light. The voices grew louder. Daniel turned his flashlight off and crept forward slowly. As he neared the end of his tunnel, he saw Tate and then Michael, Madison, Clare, and William.

Daniel realized that he must have somehow traveled parallel to and then over the cavern in his tunnel. Somehow, he was almost close enough to his friends to reach out and touch them.

Daniel also realized that his tunnel and the cavern were so dark that the others couldn't see him even if he crouched very close to the opening. He was unsure of what to do; many thoughts raced through his mind.

Michael looked at the river, which now appeared to be moving at a high rate of speed. Tate noticed it also.

"Where's he at?" muttered Tate, growing nervous that Joe had yet to resurface from the river.

"It must be raining really hard outside. The water level is getting higher," said Madison.

William looked around the cavern. "Well, it looks like it's going to keep right on rising," he said, pointing to the water-marks high on the cavern walls, just under the cavern roof.

Tate did not look happy.

Daniel stayed hidden in his tunnel while he considered his options. I could jump out and push the man into the water, he thought. Maybe I could make noise here in the tunnel and cause a distraction so that the others could run... No. What if I get caught? Or worse, what if he shoots me?

Finally, Daniel decided that he would jump out of the tunnel, push Tate into the water, and then he and the others could run. Daniel got into position and told himself he would go on three. One...two...three...nothing.

"This time for sure," he told himself. One...two...three...again nothing.

Daniel was frozen. He could not move for fear of what might happen. Then he told himself to think of the brave boy in the wall drawings.

Suddenly, Daniel's faced tightened with a look of determination. He darted out the tunnel at full speed, with his head down, running straight at Tate.

Andrew started into the tunnel that the old man had said would lead to his friends, and it wasn't long before he could see the tunnel's end and hear voices. As he neared the end of his tunnel and could see the cavern, he spotted his friends and Tate downriver. Suddenly, he saw Daniel come running out of a small tunnel behind Tate, who stood at the edge of the water. Daniel, running at full speed with his head down, barreled headfirst into Tate's stomach. Tate let out an *oomph* as Daniel made contact.

Daniel was moving so fast and with so much fury that he could not stop, and he and Tate flew off the edge of the embankment into the swift-moving river.

"Daniel!" shouted Andrew as he ran from his tunnel. Confused, the group of friends looked at Andrew and then at Daniel and Tate hitting the water. It was too late to act.

Tate and Daniel untangled themselves from each other in the water. Tate looked very frightened. He swung his arms wildly, trying to pull himself toward the shore, but the heavy current was making it difficult. Daniel was just downriver behind Tate and was making progress toward the river's bank. Suddenly, Tate lost his footing and, with one last lunge, grabbed hold of Daniel's shirt, pulling him from the edge of the river. They both disappeared under the water just before they reached the wall.

Tate and Daniel were gone.

"What do we do?" shouted Madison frantically. "We have to help Daniel!"

"I'll go after him," volunteered Michael, removing his backpack.

"No! Wait!" shouted Andrew as he made his way to the group and grabbed Michael by his sweatshirt. "The water is too high and moving too fast now. You heard Tate. He can't swim, so he's probably done for. Let's get out of here and find help." The group all stared back at Andrew, not sure what to do next.

"Listen," added Andrew. "Daniel is a good swimmer. Maybe he can make it to the edge and crawl out on the other side of the wall. We don't know how many more of those guys are around, and we're not going to be any help to Daniel if we just get caught again. We need to go find help and come back for him."

"He's right," said Clare, turning and looking at Madison and Michael and then back at Andrew.

The group stared at Andrew, and he knew what his friends were thinking. "I know the way out," he stated confidently.

Andrew turned and began to move upstream. As he led his friends through the cavern, he told them about the old man and how he had found the rest of the group.

They reached the opening and entered the tunnel. Andrew continued to lead them quickly through a series of left and right turns, and within a short time, they were in a large room that was reinforced with heavy wooden beams on all four sides.

The friends gasped as they looked around the room. What lay before them amazed and scared them all. Scattered around the room were large wooden chests.

They were open and piled high with gold nuggets. Near the chests lay skeletons in various positions.

William broke the silence. "I guess we weren't the first to try to find this gold."

"I think we should keep moving and get out of here before we join them," Michael said with urgency in his voice.

At this point, the gold and the riches it promised were the last thing on their minds. Right now, getting out and finding Daniel were their main objectives.

"There should be a way up from this room," Andrew said, surveying the walls and ceiling.

"Look! Over in the corner," Andrew said, his voice rising with excitement.

In the darkest corner of the room, a set of steep wooden stairs led to a trap door above.

The group quickly climbed the creaking stairs and pushed the trap door open. Andrew was the last, and as he waited for the others to climb the stairs, he reached into one of the chests, picked up a small gold nugget, and put it into his pocket. As they climbed through the door, they entered another small, dark room.

As the team surveyed the room, Andrew looked to his right and noticed something familiar. "Over here!" he said excitedly as he moved to a wall. "It's a dumbwaiter."

The group joined Andrew at the wall as he slid open the dumbwaiter door and reached in to grab the dangling ropes. "We can pull the dumbwaiter shelf down and get back to the kitchen one at a time."

14

THE CHASE

Once Daniel hit the water, he knew he was in trouble. The current was swift, and the water was very cold. He tried desperately to swim to one of the banks, but it took all his energy just to keep his head above water. He had been pulled under the wall and was now moving quickly through the cavern in which he and his friends had found the gold.

Suddenly, he felt himself being pulled from below. Daniel felt powerless. The undercurrent was so swift and strong that it pulled him below. Daniel fought to swim to the surface, but it was of no use. The current pushed and pulled him, and he slammed into rocks on the bottom of the river. Daniel's mind raced. He began to panic as his lungs ached for air. Just as he felt the overwhelming need to take a breath, he was catapulted upward to the surface.

The loud sound of rushing water was the first thing he noticed, and his mind struggled to make sense of the situation. Gasping for air, he pushed his head as far up as he could and filled his lungs as he was carried along by the swift-moving river. When his mind cleared, he realized that he was outdoors in the wash, which was close to overflowing its banks. It was raining very hard.

Swimming hard and trying to work with the current, Daniel struggled toward the side of the wash to grab at the roots and branches of the trees and bushes. After several misses, he was finally able to grab a branch. Slowly, Daniel pulled himself from the rushing water. When he was safe, Daniel rolled onto his back, exhausted and breathing hard.

Back in the tunnels below the old mansion, the water level of the underground river was rising very fast due to the heavy rain. The river had pushed over its bank and was now filling the lower-level tunnels.

One by one, the group climbed into the dumbwaiter and pulled themselves up. Andrew went first, followed by Madison, Clare, William, and Michael.

When Michael finally reached the others and stepped out of the dumbwaiter, he noticed that they were not in the kitchen but rather in another small, dark room. There were no doors and no windows—just a small, dark opening in one of the four walls.

"What's through there?" asked Michael, pointing at it.

"We didn't look yet," replied William.

Andrew dropped to his knees and carefully stuck his head into the opening, which was just big enough to crawl through.

"It's the fireplace," he stated, somewhat confused. "We're in a room behind the ballroom fireplace!"

Andrew climbed through the opening, and the rest of the group followed. When they emerged, they were covered in soot and ash from the fireplace.

"OK, then. Let's get out of here and get the police," Michael said to his friends, who all looked grim and scared.

At that moment, Andrew felt something behind him. He spun around and bumped into the chest of a very wet, very angry Joe!

"Well, well. Trying to skip out on Joe, eh?" he sneered. "I really don't think I can let you do that. You see, I saw the gold, and it's mine. And no snot-nosed bunch of juvenile delinquents is going to keep me from what's mine. You all should never have—"

Before Joe could finish his sentence, Michael dashed past him and headed up the large staircase.

Joe looked unsure of what to do. He lunged at Michael but missed badly, falling to the floor and dropping his kerosene lamp. As he jumped to his feet, he took one step toward the stairway and then looked back at the remaining friends. Undecided, he stood still for a long moment.

Then he shouted, "You can't get out, boy! Joe's gonna get you and break your neck!"

Overcome by anger, Joe forgot about the others and the lamp he had dropped. He headed after Michael, taking the stairs three at a time.

The kerosene from the lamp seeped into a puddle on the floor. Within seconds, the flame of the lantern ignited the kerosene and then the large, heavy drapes caught fire. The blaze spread quickly from one curtain to the next.

"Now what!" shouted William with panic in his voice.

"We run!" commanded Madison. "That's exactly what Michael wanted us to do when he got Joe to chase him."

Not needing any encouragement, the boys and girls ran toward the hallway and the front door.

Daniel finally caught his breath. He stood up on the bank of the wash and looked around, trying to figure out where he was. He could see a row of houses approximately two hundred yards ahead. The river had carried him to a place where the wash was bordered on both sides by empty fields. He looked back, but he could not see the mansion.

Daniel ran as fast as he could across the field toward the closest houses. His lungs hurt, and his breathing was once again heavy as he made it to the back fence of the first house. He jumped the fence that surrounded the property and ran to the street in front of the house.

He stood for a moment in the pouring rain, not sure if he should try to make it into town or simply knock on the door of one of the houses and ask the occupants to call for help. At that moment, Daniel saw headlights. A patrol car was coming down the street toward him.

Daniel ran toward the car, waving his hands over his head. The patrol car stopped, and Daniel ran to the driver's-side window, which, by now, the police officer had lowered.

"I need help!" shouted Daniel before the officer could ask him why he was out in the rain at five thirty in the morning.

"My friends and I went into Old Man Wilson's mansion to find gold, and we ran into some men who were there for the same reason. They were gonna kill us. I know they were gonna kill us," continued Daniel, speaking very quickly. "I don't know if my friends are still in the mansion or in the tunnels."

"The tunnels?" asked the officer, sounding confused.

"Yeah, there are tunnels under the mansion—tons of them. And tons of gold too!"

"Get in," commanded the officer.

On the way, Daniel quickly explained what had happened. The officer radioed the information to the station, including the names of Daniel and his friends, as he drove to the mansion. Within minutes, the patrol car pulled up in front of the mansion, followed by two more patrol cars.

"Stay in the car," the officer ordered Daniel and then he got out of the car.

Back in the tunnels below the old mansion, the underground river was continuing to rise quickly, filling the cavern and lower-level tunnels. The river was now moving extremely fast, pushing on the old wooden beams that supported the tunnels. The timbers creaked and cracked under the force of the rushing water.

Upstairs, Michael ran down the long hallway that led to the bedrooms. He chose the third door on the left, opened it, stepped inside, and closed it. The room was big for a bedroom—thirty feet by twenty feet—with a fireplace on one wall, cabinets and a dresser against another, and a large canopy bed against the far wall by the windows.

Like the rest of the mansion, the room was a mess, with papers and trash strewn across the floor.

Michael ran to the window to the right of the bed. He tried to push it open, but it wouldn't budge. He pushed harder on the old wood. Still nothing. It was jammed.

He jumped onto the bed and tried the window on the other side. He pushed hard on the window frame. It, too, was jammed. Michael turned to look for something to throw through the window. He saw a chair in the corner of the room.

This will do the trick, he thought, grabbing the chair. He hurled it directly at a window.

Crash! The old wood and glass splintered and shattered into hundreds of small pieces. The loud sound of rain filled the room. Gusting wind blew the sheer, white curtains upward; it picked up the papers and flung them around the room.

Michael was about to climb through the window when a large hand grabbed the back of his neck and yanked him toward the door.

"I told you that you wouldn't get away from me," snarled Joe. "Nobody messes with me, boy! Nobody!" The large, angry-looking man swung at Michael, his heavy fist connecting with Michael's shoulder and knocking him to the hardwood floor.

Madison, Clare, Andrew, and William reached the front door and opened it, feeling the sudden onslaught of hard, cold rain and wind. They quickly stepped outside and began running down the long, overgrown walkway toward the front gate and the street.

Daniel saw his friends from the front seat of the patrol car. He opened the door and jumped out. "Hey!" Daniel shouted to three officers, dressed in rain slickers, who stood next to one of the patrol cars. "Over here!"

Daniel ran to his friends. They met next to the front gate, and they all grabbed and hugged him.

"Where is Michael?" Daniel shouted over the pounding rain and wind.

"He's inside, upstairs. Joe's after him!" Madison replied just as loudly.

The officers had now arrived. They heard the last comments and directed their attention to Madison.

"Now, what exactly is going on?" asked one of the officers.

Before Madison could answer, they were all surprised by the sound of crashing glass as a chair flew through a second-floor window.

Michael lay on the floor. Joe reached down and wrapped his large hands around the boy's neck. Michael felt the man's hands tighten and his body rise as Joe began to pick him up by the neck. Suddenly, there was a flash of bright, blinding light. As quickly as Joe's hands had tightened around Michael's neck, they released. Michael fell to the floor as he heard Joe gasp in fear.

It took a couple of seconds for Michael's eyes to adjust after the flash, and when his vision cleared, he saw Joe looking as frightened as a man can look. His face was white with fear, and his eyes were wide. He was backing up with his hands out in front of him.

"No! No!" shouted Joe as a large man wearing a flannel shirt and jeans moved closer to him. Joe continued backing up.

Michael froze in his tracks, watching the old man step ever so calmly toward Joe.

"Noooo!" shouted Joe as he stepped backward. He stumbled slightly and then fell backward out the broken window, crashing to the lawn below.

The crash of the window had startled the group of friends and the officers outside the mansion. They looked up toward the second floor just in time to see a large man falling. He landed with a loud thump on the soggy earth.

"Let's go!" shouted one of the officers, and they hurried up the walkway toward the house.

Daniel, William, Madison, Clare, and Andrew followed.

Back upstairs, the old man turned his attention from the broken window to Michael and smiled.

"You're all right now, Michael," the old man said.

Michael was confused but not afraid. The old man had helped him. He did not seem to be a threat. "How do you know my name?" Michael asked suspiciously.

"I've been waiting for some time for you to come looking," said the old man, "but it's best that you leave now, before it's too late." With that, he turned around and headed for the door. Michael watched him, still confused.

When the old man reached the door, he paused for a moment and then looked over his shoulder at Michael one last time. He smiled, turned away, and stepped into the hallway.

Michael stood still for a moment, thankful that his life had been saved but still confused about what had just happened. "Hey, Mister," he called. "Wait a second!" He moved quickly from the bedroom to the hallway.

Then he gasped. "What the—"

The hallway was empty. The old man was gone.

The smell of smoke and a loud rumbling sound that seemed to shake the foundation of the house snapped Michael out of his thoughts.

What the heck is that? he wondered as he raced down the hall to the staircase. He made it to the stairs and looked over the balcony railing onto the ballroom floor. Much of the ballroom was on fire. Three police officers were at the bottom of the stairs, and his friends were coming through the front door.

At that moment, the house shook violently. From the balcony, Michael could see the floor of the ballroom break open with a billow of dust and a terrifyingly loud crack. Suddenly, a crack formed in the wall next to Michael and traveled up to the ceiling. The sounds of old pipes rattling and bursting filled the air, followed by more loud moans, cracks, creaks, and rattles.

"Get out of here!" shouted Michael to the police and his friends "I'm OK! Let's go!" he urged, taking the stairs three at a time.

The whole house seemed to be moaning and moving now, as the water-filled tunnels and caverns began to collapse, weakening the house's foundation.

The entire group ran for the door, stumbling as the house began to move and shake more violently by the second. They piled out the door into the rain and ran toward the patrol cars.

As they reached the first car, they heard a series of loud cracks, pops, and moans, which turned into a rumbling crash as the house began to sink and collapse into the earth.

"What the—" one of the officers started to say but was cut off by another loud crash as the mansion sank further into the ground as its foundation gave way to the turbulence beneath it. The walls collapsed inward, and the windows on all three floors began to burst, sending shards of wood and glass into the yard. Flames began to rise from the house as the gas pipes broke and the fire that engulfed the ballroom ignited the gas.

"There's an old man inside the house!" Michael said to an officer.

"There's nothing we can do, son," the officer stated solemnly. "The house is coming down."

15

IT'S OVER

They all stood silently, facing the collapsing house, as the fire inside began to reach through the windows and cracks, only to be pushed back inside by the wind and rain. One of the officers had returned to his car and was on the radio.

Andrew broke the silence. "It's over," he said.

As they stood together watching the house burn, Michael slid his hands into his back pockets and felt something. As he pulled the folded paper from his pocket, he realized it was the map.

"Daniel," he called.

Daniel turned. Michael smiled and showed him the map. Daniel returned the smile. Michael unfolded the map and turned it slowly in his hands, looking at the drawings in the corners. Astonished, he called out to his friends, "Look at this!"

Michael held up the map for the others to see. As he shifted the map in his hands, the patterns in the corners aligned with the mountains that were now visible behind the ruins of the mansion.

"The patterns are the real mystery of the map," stated Andrew. "They line up with the mountains, where the gold is coming from. What we found was probably just runoff."

"Does that means the real source of the gold might still be up in those mountains?" asked William.

"Seems so. And the lines inside these shapes might just be a map of caves like the ones below the mansion," Michael responded, leaning forward and looking closely at the map.

"Maybe we should save that adventure for another night," Andrew said with a tired smile.

His friends looked back at him, suddenly aware of all the things that had happened to them that night and feeling as tired as he looked. Behind Andrew, the friends could see a car's headlights and then another set. Within minutes, the mansion was a bustling scene as the town's fire engines, ambulance, and additional patrol cars arrived. Shortly thereafter, their parents arrived in separate cars.

Andrew saw his father's car pull up to the curb. His father looked worried as he dashed toward the crowd of emergency personnel.

"Dad!" shouted Andrew. "Over here!"

Andrew could hear the exhaustion in his own voice. Andrew's father ran toward him, grabbed him, and hugged him for a long time.

Daniel's father was the last of the parents to arrive. As he approached Daniel, he looked relieved to see his son, but his face quickly turned stern.

"You have a lot of explaining to do," he stated.

Daniel stood as tall as he could and looked straight back at his father. "I'm OK, Dad," he said, his voice carrying a hint of sarcasm. Then, without sarcasm, he added, "I know I have a lot to explain."

Daniel's father looked somewhat surprised and a little embarrassed for not showing concern, although Daniel knew that deep inside, his father did care about him. Daniel's father hugged him and then whispered, "I'm sorry." The apology was meant for Daniel, but everyone close by heard it.

The chief of police came over to the group. Andrew and Michael quickly explained what had happened, starting with the map and the plan and eventually getting to the discovery of the gold, Joe, Tate, and the old man.

With the house settled and the fire extinguished, the emergency-services personnel began to move in on the house to get a better look.

It was a long night for the six friends, and throughout the morning, each would tell his or her story in detail to family members and the police.

Andrew and his father left the scene at seven in the morning. His father asked him several more questions, and when they arrived home, Andrew's mother was waiting in the kitchen.

She hugged Andrew and told him to take a warm bath. Her voice carried a hint of the coming punishment, but Andrew knew she had been worried. "I'll make you some breakfast," she called after him.

Then she slid over to hug her husband. "How about some coffee?" she asked him.

"That would be great," he replied. "I have a story to write."

That day, the local newspaper released a special late edition. A bold headline on the front page blared, "GOLD DISCOVERED IN TELANE."

Over the next couple of days, the town of Telane was very much alive and excited. Everyone in town was talking about the six friends and the evening they spent in and below the mansion.

There were many theories, but the friends all agreed that the best one was that Theodore Wilson had discovered the tunnels while building the secret room behind his fireplace. Perhaps he dug a little too deeply, opening up the ground below him. He had explored the caves, found the gold, and mapped the location. Then he had somehow determined that more gold was still hidden deep in the mountains. He probably built the dumbwaiter as a means of transporting the gold from the tunnels without revealing his secret and risking that others would try to take what was his.

The group agreed that Theodore seemed to have had a great sense of adventure and planned to give the map to his sons so that they could appreciate the wonder and amazement of discovering the gold for the very first time.

Unfortunately, Theodore died of a heart attack one evening before he was able to share his secret with anyone.

The townspeople figured that Native Americans originally had discovered the caverns and may have even lived in them, which explained the cave drawings.

It was still anyone's guess as to how the tunnels were dug, but it seemed logical that during the initial discovery of gold in the region in the 1800s, someone had located the treasure by following the river upstream from its mouth at the ocean.

This theory seemed reasonable because every so often, people found small nuggets of gold off the coast of Telane. Those finds usually were attributed to the many sunken ships that lay just off the rocky coastline. But the river must have carried those nuggets from inside the caverns after heavy rainstorms, just like the one that had brought down the mansion.

It would have taken a lot of courage to follow the river upstream. The prospectors would have had to swim underground into the caverns, not knowing for sure whether the caverns actually existed or whether there would be air to breathe inside. But the lure of gold was strong, and someone was always willing to risk his or her life for fortune.

The townspeople also theorized that once a brave prospector had found the gold, ruthless people who were willing to kill for treasure discovered his secret—hence the skeletons in the tunnels. It was likely that the last person with knowledge of the gold had died in the caves, and with Theodore's death, the secret was buried.

What no one in town could believe—and the friends had been careful not to say much about—was the old man they had encountered in the tunnels. Most speculated that it was Old Man Wilson himself. Some thought he was a homeless person taking shelter in the mansion. Perhaps he was a partner of Joe and Tate but decided that he didn't want the young friends to be harmed.

Regardless of how the theories played out, Andrew and Michael knew what they had encountered. But it was their secret, and they made a pact that they would only share it with the group that had entered the house.

16

IMAGINATION PARK

Word of the events spread quickly to nearby towns, and then the story went nationwide. Telane came back to life and recaptured its prosperity as the media, treasure seekers, the curious, and tourists filled local hotels, inns, restaurants, and shops. The gold rush seemed to be making a comeback in Telane, and local merchants sold "Gold Rush '99" T-shirts and souvenirs.

The local hardware-store owner said he couldn't stock enough shovels, picks, and gold-mining equipment as prospectors once again headed into the hills to find elusive treasures. All the local businesses seemed to experience new prosperity.

One late afternoon, a man dressed in a suit arrived at Michael's door and began speaking to his mom. Michael heard him say something about the Wilson estate.

BERNARD LUTHI

Michael hurried to the phone and called Andrew. "Get over here, now," he quickly whispered. "There's some lawyer here talking about Old Man Wilson."

Andrew hurried over, and when he arrived, Michael opened the door and let him in. Inside the front room, Michael's mother and sister were sitting on the couch. Across from them sat a slightly overweight middle-aged man of average height with short gray hair. He wore an expensive-looking business suit; a very white, pressed shirt; and a dark-blue tie. On the coffee table in front of him lay several papers, spread out neatly, along with his open briefcase.

Andrew shot a worried glance at Michael, remembering what happened the last time a man in a suit was in Michael's house.

"Don't worry," Michael whispered with a sly grin. "No one's getting arrested this time."

Michael quietly caught Andrew up on the conversation. The man was the lawyer who had been handling the affairs of John Wilson—or Old Man Wilson, as the townspeople referred to him.

Apparently, Old Man Wilson hadn't died in the house after all; in fact, he had recently passed away in Florida. It seemed that someone or something had scared him in the mansion one evening, and he had grabbed what he could carry and moved to Florida, leaving the house unattended. For the past several years, Old Man Wilson had lived quietly and happily near a beach in a nice trailer park in Florida, soaking up the sun.

112

Michael and his family were the heirs to the property.

The lawyer read several paragraphs from one of the documents, and then he stopped and looked up at Michael's mother. "It seems that you have sole ownership of not only the house and land but also what's beneath it, and that includes the mining rights."

"The gold," Michael whispered loudly as he looked over at Andrew.

"Yes, that would include the gold," stated the lawyer matter-of-factly. "I just need your signatures here," he said to Michael's mother. "We'll get this recorded with the city, and you can take possession of the property."

Andrew looked over at Michael and smiled. Michael was grinning from ear to ear, looking at his mom, who sat quietly with her mouth open in disbelief and eyes tearing up with happiness.

Weeks after the lawyer's visit, when all the paperwork was signed and finalized, Michael's family donated a large portion of the Wilson Manor land to the city. They donated the land to south of the mansion to the area's Native American tribe. Michael's mother said that her family was blessed to have received such an unexpected gift, and it was only fair to do right by others. That included giving the sacred land back to the tribe.

Michael's mom was also generous with the friends who had ventured into the mansion that night, including the boys, Madison, and Clare. They would not have to worry about college tuition or even buying their first cars. In fact, none of the children's parents would need to worry about finances for the rest of their lives.

The land and some cash were donated to the city for one specific purpose: to build and maintain a city park, concert venue, and recreation center that the town could be proud of. Over the next several weeks, the overgrown land was transformed into a wonderful park with picnic tables, swings, monkey bars, and a stage. The main attractions were the modern sports fields, including a baseball diamond that would rival any in the state.

Simultaneously, a local history exhibit was being constructed that would include a section that celebrated the history of Telane, from its Native American roots through its gold rushes, including the recent one.

The first baseball game at the new park attracted thousands of townspeople and visitors. It was a great day, with a parade in the morning and a festival with food booths, games, and carnival rides throughout the day. There was even a fireworks show that evening.

The park was aptly named "Imagination Park" in honor of Theodore Wilson.

The first batter in the first game played at the new park was Daniel. He stood very tall and confident that day, something he had been doing since the night the friends spent in the mansion. His friends had noticed the change in him right away, and so had everyone else.

William stood in the batter's box, waiting for his turn at bat. "Knock it outta the park, you madman!" he shouted to Daniel, who looked back at him and smiled coyly.

William still had his sense of humor, and he had a field day with the reporters and television crews that had come to interview the boys. William had become something of a national celebrity. He was even a guest on a daytime talk show. It seemed that he had a career in show business in his future.

Andrew stood at the entrance to the dugout, putting on his batting gloves and getting ready to step into the on-deck circle after Daniel's turn at bat. He felt good. Everything seemed to have worked out for the best.

He scanned the crowd and noticed his dad sitting close behind home plate, scribbling on a pad of paper. Covering the events for tomorrow's edition of the *Telane Tribune*, no doubt, thought Andrew. He smiled.

The events in town and the renewed excitement had revived something in Andrew's father. Once again, he was busy writing a book. Andrew had no doubt that this time, his father would finish writing his book and publish it.

Sitting next to Andrew's father was Madison. She turned toward Andrew and caught his glance. She smiled, and it was more than just a friendly smile. Andrew felt even better.

The first pitch of the game came screaming toward Daniel. He took a mighty swing and connected with a crack, sending the ball flying skyward toward the old water tower that still stood at the edge of the baseball field. It was the lone reminder of the mansion, which had been torn down and removed.

There wasn't any question as the ball flew over the outfield fence. "Going, going, gone! It's a home run!" the announcer exclaimed over the loudspeakers as Daniel headed for first base, pumping his fist in the air.

The ball flew over the tall outfield fence and rolled to a stop just short of a tractor that belonged to the mining company hired by Michael's family to extract dirt, rocks, and gold from the earth.

ABOUT THE AUTHOR

Bernard Luthi is a lifelong fan of coming-of-age mystery adventures, from the Hardy Boys novels to classic films such as The Goonies. His own childhood daydreams about lost treasure inspired his first novel, Midnight, Ghosts, and Gold!

A native of Los Angeles, Luthi lives in the San Gabriel Valley and is married with two college-age sons. He enjoys a successful professional life in technology and e-commerce.

Made in the USA
San Bernardino, CA
20 November 2015